CAST

Miss Agatha Burman. Aft
the family home into a boa
keeping it spotlessly clean.

Em. Her cook. According to her father's will, Agatha has to keep her on forever. She's a superb cook but her slovenly ways grate on Agatha's delicate nerves.

Fred Slupper. Agatha's handyman and gardener, who revered her father and respects the old house in ways that Em does not.

Dr. Allen Gremson. One of Agatha's boarders, a young doctor who maintains his offices on the ground floor.

Mirrie Jodson. His efficient office nurse, a platinum-haired gold-digger who also boards with Agatha.

Julia Rost. Another boarder, an attractive, good-natured widow who owns an interior decorating shop nearby.

Mr. Appely. A boarder who owns a book and greeting-card shop just down the street. He has the only television set in the house.

Dr. Christine Herser. A newly minted doctor and the most recently arrived boarder, who also has offices on the ground floor. She was formerly engaged to Allen, but he didn't approve of women doctors.

Will Kroning. Em's nephew and Mirrie's beau. If he really will have the money he says he will inherit someday, he's definitely husband material despite his coarse ways.

Ginny Kroning. His sister, a flighty little thing.

Mrs. Mabel Kroning. Their outspoken mother, who rivals Agatha when it comes to house cleaning.

Inspector Lewis. The detective on the case. He was called Stinky Lewis in grade school, where he knew Will. He also admires Mirrie.

Books by Constance & Gwenyth Little

The Grey Mist Murders (1938)*
Black-Headed Pins (1938)*
The Black Gloves (1939)*
Black Corridors (1940)*
The Black Paw (1941)*
The Black Shrouds (1941)*
The Black Thumb (1942)*
The Black Rustle (1943)*
The Black Honeymoon (1944)*
Great Black Kanba (1944)*
The Black Eye (1945)*
The Black Stocking (1946)*
The Black Goatee (1947)*
The Black Coat (1948)*
The Black Piano (1948)*
The Black House (1950)*
The Black Smith (1950)*
The Blackout (1951)
The Black Dream (1952)*
The Black Iris (1953)
The Black Curl (1953)

*reprinted by the Rue Morgue Press
as of December 2005

The Black Dream

by Constance & Gwenyth Little

Rue Morgue Press

Lyons / Boulder

The Black Dream
Copyright © 1952, 1980
Reprinted with the permission of
the authors' estate.

New material copyright © 2005
by The Rue Morgue Press

ISBN: 0-915230-87-9

Any resemblance to persons living or dead
would be downright ridiculous.

Printed at Johnson Printing
Boulder, Colorado

The Rue Morgue Press
P.O. Box 4119
Boulder, CO 80306

PRINTED IN THE UNITED STATES OF AMERICA

About the Littles

Although all but one of their books had "black" in the title, the 21 mysteries of Constance (1899-1980) and Gwenyth (1903-1985) Little were far from somber affairs. The two Australian-born sisters from East Orange, New Jersey, were far more interested in coaxing chuckles than in inducing chills from their readers.

Indeed, after their first book, *The Grey Mist Murders*, appeared in 1938, Constance rebuked an interviewer for suggesting that their murders weren't realistic by saying, "Our murderers strangle. We have no sliced-up corpses in our books." However, as the books mounted, the Littles did go in for all sorts of gruesome murder methods—"horrible," was the way their own mother described them—which included the occasional sliced-up corpse.

But the murders were always off stage and tempered by comic scenes in which bodies and other objects, including swimming pools, were constantly disappearing and reappearing. The action took place in large old mansions, boarding houses, hospitals, hotels, or on trains or ocean liners, anywhere the Littles could gather together a large cast of eccentric characters, many of whom seemed to have escaped from a Kaufman play or a Capra movie. The typical Little heroine—each book was a stand-alone—often fell under suspicion herself and turned detective to keep the police from slapping the cuffs on. Whether she was a working woman or a spoiled little rich brat, she always spoke her mind, kept her rather sarcastic sense of humor, and got her man, both murderer and husband. But if marriage was in the offing, it was always on her terms and the vows were taken with more than a touch of cynicism. Love was grand, but it was even grander if the husband could either pitch in with the cooking and cleaning or was wealthy enough to hire household help.

The Littles wrote all their books in bed—"Chairs give one backaches," Gwenyth complained—with Constance providing detailed plot outlines while Gwenyth did the final drafts. Over the years that pattern changed somewhat, but Constance always insisted that Gwen "not mess up my clues." Those clues were everywhere, and the Littles made sure there were no loose ends. Seemingly irrelevant events were revealed to be of major significance in the final summation. The plots were often preposterous, a fact often recognized by both the Littles and their characters, all of whom seem to be winking at the reader, almost as if sharing a private joke. You just have to accept the fact that there are different natural laws in the wacky universe created by these sisters. There are no other mystery writers quite like them. At times, their books seem to be an odd collaboration between P.G. Wodehouse and Cornell Woolrich.

The Littles published their two final novels, *The Black Curl* and *The Black Iris*, in 1953, and if they missed writing after that, they were at least able to devote more time to their real passion—traveling. The two made at least three trips around the world at a time when that would have been a major undertaking. For more information on the Littles and their books, see the introductions by Tom & Enid Schantz to The Rue Morgue Press editions of *The Black Gloves* and *The Black Honeymoon*.

Chapter One

MISS AGATHA BUNSON found herself polishing the stair rail rather too vigorously and realized that she was thinking of her father again. She must stop it, put it out of her mind. It always made her angry, and it was silly and futile.

She heard her cook, Em, slapping pots around in the kitchen in preparation for lunch, and her hand dropped limply to her side. She couldn't stand it—she *couldn't*. That dirty Em, dropping water and bits of food all over the place—it was absolutely disgusting. And when she cleaned up the kitchen after the creature she felt almost sick. Three times a day she had to go into that kitchen and clean up the slop, and it was really dreadful.

Agatha found that she was shaking a little with pure fury. Couldn't Em *see* how dirty she was, how dirty the kitchen was after she had left it? Scraps of food left on the dishes, and streaks of grease on the tables?

Oh, if she could only get rid of the woman! How could her father have done such a thing to her, leaving a will that bound her to support Em and Fred? Of course Fred was all right, really. She needed a gardener and handyman, and although he made her uneasy when he came into the house, he was not in too often, and he kept the cellar spick and span. He lived in a room over the garage, and she paid him a small salary, as she did Em. It was not much in either case, but it was all she could afford, and it wasn't fair. She was supposed to take care of these two people, and yet her father had left her nothing but the house and a little cash. She'd had to arrange her own income by renting some of the rooms and serving meals to the doctor and a few others who came in. Em was a good cook, of course—she had never tried to deny that—but so *dirty*. If she could only get rid of Em she'd do the cooking herself and not be so extravagant about it, either, and she could save the salary as well.

She began to rub the stair rail in a burst of furious energy until she reached the bottom, when she swept into the kitchen and stalked over to the sink. She carefully washed out the rag she had been using and hung it up to dry.

Em ignored her, but hoped privately that she wouldn't hang around. Interfering people were a pest and a nuisance when she was trying to cook.

Agatha turned from the sink with her fingers curled tightly into her palms.

"Em."

Em had a reputation for being hard of hearing, and she continued to stir something in a pot without raising her eyes.

Anger sharpened Agatha's voice, and she repeated more loudly, "Em! I'm talking to you."

Em continued to stir. "O.K., O.K. I'm listening. You don't have to blast the ears offa me."

Agatha carefully uncurled her fingers and tried to make her voice reasonable and persuasive. "You know, you're very foolish to stay here. I can't pay you much, and you'd make three times the salary somewhere else."

Em tasted her mixture with the stirring spoon, while Agatha averted her eyes. "No use you startin' that again. I'm stayin' here. I like it here. And what do you mean, 'three times the salary'? You mean four or five times. Anyways, why should I bother to make more money, which I don't never use? My niece and nephew would only spend it foolish after I die. I'm comfortable and I'm staying, get it?"

Agatha got it, and left the kitchen without another word.

Em glanced at the clock, and decided that she'd better hurry a little. The doctor was due at any minute, and his office hours would start in an hour. She hoped, as she always did, that he'd get back in time to eat a proper lunch. So often he was late and had to skimp, or miss the meal entirely. It seemed a shame, when he had to pay for the food whether he ate it or not.

The doctor was in good time that day, as it happened. He felt so leisurely that he stood outside Agatha's house for a few minutes and ran a speculative eye over its proportions.

It was a large house, square, with four tremendous, fluted columns rising to the top, and it stood close to the pavement. Shops nudged it on either side, and the original white paint had faded to a shabby gray. Dr. Gremson glanced at his own neat sign tacked to one of the columns, and sighed a little. If the woman would only have the place painted! She was thoroughly neurotic, rarely went out, and was concerned only with the inside of her house. It was really absurd, the contrast of the neglected exterior with the gleaming cleanliness of the interior.

As he went in, he made a sudden decision. He'd have the house painted himself. It would be well worth it to him. He was established here, and the rooms were large with plenty of space for his equipment, and the waiting room and offices were dignified and looked expensive.

He went into the dining room and admired its beauty, as he had done many times before. It faced the back, with an outlet through a large bay window. The view was nothing but the rear of buildings on the next street, but there was a small yard between with an overlarge tree in its center. The furniture was mellow old mahogany, which Agatha's father had loved and cherished. Two crystal chandeliers hung from the ceiling over the long table, and they sparkled with a multitude of colors. They were always clean, to the last, glittering crystal drop.

Seven places had been set at the table, and as the doctor walked in, he saw that two of them were occupied. His office nurse, Mirrie Jodson, was there, and she gave him a bright smile. Platinum-blond hair, mask of makeup from hairline to neck, and a brightly colored handkerchief fanning out from the pocket of her white uniform. Dr. Gremson was conscious of familiarity in the wish that she looked a little less flashy, but reminded himself, as he had done before, that she was a most efficient assistant.

He nodded at Julia Rost, who sat in the other occupied place. She was a widow who ran the interior-decorating shop next door, a successful makeover from her late husband's languishing upholstering business. In her way she was as flashy as Mirrie, but she'd had more experience, and the end result was smoother. Her hair, produced from a different bottle, was red, and it was drawn into something attractive at the back. It had more sophistication, Dr. Gremson thought, than the curls that rioted over Mirrie's head and down her neck. The makeup was more restrained, too, although he was prepared to guess that it took quite as long to apply.

"Hi, Allen. How are you?" Julia asked easily.

Mirrie looked down at her plate and gritted her teeth. Why should that henna-haired old bag be allowed to call him by his first name when she was obliged to say "Dr. Gremson" at all times? She knew him much better than Julia Rost did, and she'd like to see him get along without her, too.

Em came in and put a filled plate carefully before the doctor. "Now, you take your time and eat it, hear me? Don't be running off to your office with your stomach half empty. I have something nice for your dessert when you've finished that."

Julia glanced at Em's retreating back, and grinned ruefully. "We get cheated here, Mirrie. We pay the same as this guy, but Em gives us the leftovers that she figures aren't good enough for him. And yet I'm kind to children and animals, and always shell out for worthy causes."

Agatha came in and took her place at the head of the table. She saw that there were three unoccupied settings and figured that Mr. Appely, who rented the little room on the second floor, must be bringing in guests. He ran a small book and greeting-card shop down the street, and he appeared presently with two business associates whom he gravely introduced to the rest of the table. Agatha was never quite happy about these occasional intruders, but of course it made a little extra money for her.

One of the guests was a youngish man, and Mirrie smiled brightly at him until he mentioned his wife, when she lost interest.

Agatha did not spend much time in the dining room. She ate her lunch quickly, murmured an excuse, and hurried back up-stairs. Mr. Appely glanced after her, took a long breath, and broke into a smile.

"Miss Mirrie, I have a greeting card at the shop—just came in this morning, an angel's head, you know, and I do really think you must have been the model. So like you."

Mirrie smirked, murmured that she had no time to model for angels, and wished that Mr. Appely were not short, plump, and middle-aged.

Mr. Appely went on gaily, "No, I mean it. You saw that card, Bill, and isn't it a portrait of Miss Mirrie?"

Bill produced a smile that suggested a mind occupied with something else, and at the same time Em walked into the room.

She looked first toward the head of the table, and nodded. "I see she's gorn. Well, I'll take a bit of a rest in her chair, here, while I see if you all got enough to eat."

"Excellent meal, as usual," Allen said amiably.

Julia raised an eyebrow in Em's direction. "It's always excellent for him, but all I ever get is the edges. The stuff was a bit burned today, too."

Em folded her hands over her stomach. "It's your tongue that's burned, with all them cocktails you swill."

Julia laughed at her. "You can't take constructive criticism, that's your trouble. You always come in here for compliments after a meal, and it does you good to have someone tell you the truth, just for a change."

Mr. Appely's mouth had primmed into a narrow line, and he nodded. "You've no right to be taking your ease in Miss Bunson's chair. She should know that you come in here every day after she has left, like this."

Em gave him a lazy stare that brought the color into his face. She said, "Ahh, go and bury your head under a plant that you don't care nothing about."

One of Mr. Appely's guests found this highly entertaining and struggled, unsuccessfully, with a burst of laughter.

Julia cocked an ear to the door. "You'd better skip—I hear Miss Bunson coming," she lied cheerfully.

"I ain't afraid of her." But Em raised her bulk from the chair and disappeared into the kitchen with a certain amount of speed.

Actually, Agatha had gone to her room for a clean handkerchief. But the handkerchief box was not in its accustomed place in her neat drawer—and suddenly she was frightened. Twice in the last month little things had disappeared from her room—and had turned up in her small sitting room downstairs. She must go down—stop this nonsense of pounding heart and sweating palms—the handkerchief box was probably there. And there was some reasonable explanation for this thing. Stop thinking about Father—she *must* stop it.

But very clearly in her mind, she saw his face and heard the words that he had uttered almost on his deathbed.

"I shouldn't leave you running around loose, this way, Aggie. I should have put you in a comfortable home, where they could have looked after you."

Chapter 2

AGATHA shook her head a little and frowned down at her hands. It seemed almost as though Father had thought she was insane, and he'd been a doctor, too. But surely that was absurd. No one else had any doubt of her sanity. and anyway, Father had never liked her. Dhe'd always known it. He'd been fond of his younger daughter, though, and she'd disgraced herself by running away with a man. So like Father, to care for the *wrong* child. But he'd lived to learn that Agatha was the right one. She'd stayed with him and taken care of him and nursed him through his last illness to his death.

She met Em coming out of the kitchen. Em sidled past with averted eyes and gave an audible little sniff. She knew what the old bat was going to do now, just as though she didn't keep her kitchen clean enough for anybody but a half-wit scarecrow.

Agatha passed through the kitchen and into her little sitting room. The box of handkerchiefs was on the window sill, and she stood looking at it for a while with her brow furrowed. It was just this sleepwalking, and she'd have to find some way to stop it—no knowing where she'd go if it kept on. Surely she could find some method of keeping herself in her room at night. A lot of people had the same troubl. It was nothing too unusual, and surely nothing to worry about, but she'd have to think out a way of locking herself in.

She hurried out to the kitchen and busied herself with the cleaning. It did not take very long, since she did it every day, and when she had finished, she went upstairs to wax the doctor's furniture.

She was interrupted by the loud peal of the front doorbell. The bell on the back door had as strident a sound, but they were different, and she never confused them. The bell at the front was under her own name plate so that Dr. Gremson's patients would not disturb her. They were instructed by another neat sign to walk in. She didn't quite like it, but the doctor had insisted. Of course they walked through the hall only as far as the doctor's suite, and then went directly into his waiting room, but anyone could slip quietly up the stairs if he had criminal intentions of some sort.

She was favorably impressed with the young woman who stood outside the door. No hat, short dark hair, and blue eyes. Her makeup was very restrained, and she wore a plain but well-cut suit. She was attractive, though, and Agatha approved her refined appearance, so different from those two painted hussies, Julia Rost and Mirrie Jodson.

The girl smiled. "May I see the rooms you are renting?"

Agatha opened the door wide. "There are two rooms. One is quite large, as you will see."

The front room was large, as Agatha had said, but the back room was small. However, there was a large closet and a small lavatory and shower between them, one of Agatha's improvements in the house when she realized that she'd have to arrange some sort of an income for herself.

The girl prowled around, and Agatha asked, "What is your name, please?"

"I'm Dr. Christine Herser."

Agatha stared. "You're a *doctor?*"

Christine nodded absently. The place would be all right. All she had to do was to make enough to pay the rent. She could always get something to eat by dropping in on her brothers. She'd have to get some screens to put across the middle of the big room so that she'd have some space for a waiting room, and she could live in the small room at the back.

"You don't look that old, really," Agatha was saying.

"Oh." Christine gave her a vague glance. "I suppose not. It runs in my family."

Agatha accepted a deposit and went back to finish her cleaning. She was behind time and she'd have to hurry, but she was pleased. The rooms were rented, and to a doctor, which was suitable. Astonishing that the girl looked so young—Agatha knew how long it took to be a doctor.

The back door buzzed as she started up the stairs, and she clicked her tongue in annoyance. She'd have to go down again and answer it, all because Em insisted upon spending the afternoon on her slatternly back. Wasn't there *some* way to get rid of the horrid creature? Perhaps she should consult a lawyer. She ran a nervous, smoothing hand over her hair and hurried though the kitchen to the door.

It was that uncouth lout, Will Kroning, Em's nephew. Agatha let him in in dour silence, her foot tapping impatiently on the shining linoleum.

"Got a day off," he said airily. "Thought I'd look in on Aunt Em."

"Yes." Agatha sent a chilly glance at a straight kitchen chair. "Sit down, Will. I'll tell Em. I'm going up, anyway."

He sprawled in the chair and said, "Ahh, let her sleep. I got a paper here. I'll read till she gets down."

Agatha left the room with her mouth in a thin line. She would *not* let Em sleep. It would be a pleasure to wake her with a legitimate excuse. She climbed to the third floor, and anger dogged her tired legs. Em was supposed to take care of the cleaning up here, and it was simply unspeakable! Dust and dirt and disorder—she couldn't *stand* it. She'd have to come up and clean the place herself. Impossible to think of all this filth, even though she rarely came up here. No use saying anything to Em, of course. She'd get a rude reply, and that would be all. She knocked on Em's door and realized that two tears of frustrated fury had crept out of the corners of her eyes.

Em was vexed at being disturbed and said so in rather crude language, but Agatha did not wait to listen. She returned to the second floor and relieved her feelings by a frenzy of activity on the doctor's bedroom furniture.

As soon as Agatha had left the kitchen, Will cast aside his paper and crept through the front hall into Dr. Gremson's waiting room. Mirrie was not there, and three women patients discomposed him by regarding him with pale, blank eyes. He supposed that Mirrie was back with the doctor, doing unthinkable things to hapless victims, and he picked up a magazine and leaned against her desk, pretending to be absorbed in it. He knew that the three women were still gazing at him, and he felt color burning into his face. Why in hell couldn't they read, or gossip together, or spit on the floor, for Godsakes? Who ast them to sit there rubbering at him, anyways?

Mirrie returned to her desk on brisk feet and hesitated when she saw Will, frowning over the mixed feelings that she always had about him. He was a good-looking fella, you couldn't get around that, but Em's *nephew*. A relative of the *cook*. He was crude, too, and his job was ominously vague. He was in a department store, and she suspected that he carried boxes and furniture around from here to there. Certainly she wasn't sure—it was always possible that it was a decent job involving a white collar.

He mopped his brow and whispered, "Hiya, babe."

"Shh."

Will was ill at ease, as usual, in the doctor's waiting room, and he muttered urgently, "How's about stepping out tonight?"

Mirrie fingered the fancy handkerchief that sprouted from her pocket, and looked down at her neat, white feet. She had a dearth of other dates, and so she always accepted him, but she wished violently that once—just once—she could honestly inform him that she had a previous engagement.

"Well—" She sighed. "I had intended to save this evening. There are some things that I ought to do."

"Good." He grinned at her. "You can do them some other time. I got my car, so I'll visit with Em till you get outa here."

Mirrie sighed again and watched him as he slid out into the hall and shut the door quietly behind him. The telephone rang, and she put an impatient hand on it. She hoped those three patients who were sitting looking at her didn't think she was going out on a date with him. He ought to dress more conservatively and leave violent colors to the women. A dark suit, now, with his hair brushed the right way, and a tie that didn't burst out into brilliant horseshoes, and she with her blond curls and a smart dress—they'd make a nice-looking couple. If she could be sure of that job of his, too—

She answered the phone, and Julia Rost's carefully cultured voice slid smoothly into her ear. "Mirrie, my dear, do you suppose Allen will be through fairly early tonight? I have some interesting people coming in, and I want him to meet them. Tell him to drop by for a cocktail before dinner."

Mirrie relaxed the frown from her forehead because her mother had told her not to start lines growing there too early. She unconsciously aped Julia's accent and said that she'd tell the doctor when she got a chance, but she doubted whether he'd be through in time.

"Just so long as you tell him, then," Julia said cheerfully. "If he can't make it, we'll be disappointed. But I know he likes my cocktails, and I shall be making them, anyway—"

Mirrie put down the phone with a sharp click. How about herself? Didn't it occur to Julia that she'd like to meet some interesting people? She hoped she'd forget to tell the doctor.

Unfortunately, she never forgot any of the things she was supposed to tell him. It was part of her efficient handling of the job. She delivered Julia's message in a flat voice, and he said vaguely, "Oh, all right, if I have time."

He did have time, and was able even to run up to his room to freshen his appearance. He put on a red tie, brushed his sandy-colored hair, and looked at himself in the mirror. Nothing much to his face, but he had plenty of hair—wouldn't go bald in a hurry. He must get hold of Agatha and tell her he had a tenant for those rooms across the hall. now that he'd talked Gibbs into locating there. High time, too—no knowing what sort of impossible person she'd put in there if he left it to her much longer.

He went downstairs without bothering to put on a topcoat. It was April, and the weather was getting warmer, and he was only going next door. He wouldn't stop to look for Agatha now. Julia would be waiting in her carefully decorated little office, where she served cocktails or tea, according to the customer.

He reached the sidewalk and turned to glance back at Agatha's house, with the painting job in his mind, and stopped dead in his tracks.

There was another sign on one of the huge columns now, larger than his own, and his eyes widened in horror. The sign said briefly, "Christine Herser, M.D."

Chapter 3

CHRISTINE came out of the front door carrying a hammer. Her sign needed a few more nails, but when she saw Allen Gremson, she stopped, the hammer swinging loosely in her hand while a faint flush colored her face.

Allen had gone a dark red. He swallowed twice before he was able to shout, "Christine!" And then he went dumb again.

Christine swung the hammer and said, too airily, "Oh, hello, Allen. How are you?"

He pounded up the steps of the veranda and stood beside her. "What *is* this?" he demanded grimly.

"What is what?"

"You're a—a graduate M.D.?"

"With honors, I graduated."

He looked her over. "Oh yes, with honors. And now you're going to foist yourself on an unsuspecting public."

Christine raised the hammer a little and gazed wistfully at it. "I think I'm prepared," she said coldly. "No one should know better than you how long it takes to become a doctor. When did we break our engagement?"

"I—er—"

"Quite a good many years, isn't it?"

"As far as I know," Allen said stiffly, "the engagement never was broken. If you've married someone else, I think it's a case of breach of promise."

"Don't be silly. I'd been busy studying, and then I worked with Mother until she died."

"I was sorry to hear of her death," Allen said conventionally. "I sent you a note."

"No, you didn't."

"I did."

"Well, I never received it."

"Of course you received it. It was simply that among so many, it made no impression on you."

Christine extended a toe and gazed down at it. "My brother helped me—perhaps—"

"I suppose he simply threw a bunch of them away to make things easier. I wrote to you and had no answer at all."

"Sorry."

"I gather that you came here simply to make things difficult for me," Allen went on bitterly. "You must have seen my sign, and you know how I dislike having my office side by side with a woman doctor. I suppose you've rented the rooms across the hall."

"Well, yes. I did see your sign, and I have rented the rooms across the hall, but not with any idea of driving you into one of your ridiculous tempers. I rented those rooms because they happen to suit me. They are just what I want. I think it's high time you realized that women can be as skillful as men, even as doctors. Like father, like son—but times do change, you know."

"Be good enough to leave my father out of this."

"Oh yes." Christine swung the hammer in an almost ominous fashion. "There is no reason why I should tear your father down, simply because you tore my mother to pieces."

Allen was horrified, at that point, to discover that they had an audience on the sidewalk consisting of two teenage girls and a little brother who belonged to one of them. He resisted an impulse to tell them sharply to go on about their various businesses.

Christine had noticed them, too, and she hurried down the steps exclaiming, "Oh, what a dear little boy!"

The teenagers departed, after suitable smirks, with the urchin in tow, and Christine returned to the veranda. She would have passed Allen by, but he caught her arm and held it.

"How can you possibly hope to make out in a location like this? I know how much those rooms cost."

"I believe in getting into a good location to begin with. If I can't make a go of it, I'll have to look for cheaper quarters. But I'm living here too."

"You're living here?" He was astounded. "What room—"

"Right in the office. The small back room."

"You can't do that. There are only two rooms. Do you expect your waiting patients to sit and watch you pummel the victim on the table?"

Christine gave him a chilly eye. "I do *not* pummel, and my patients are not victims. I'll have screens to divide the big room."

"That's no good. If they can't see, they can hear, and that's almost as bad. The whole thing is absurd. You can't tell me that your patients don't grunt as you push the wind in and out of them. You'd better have your screens shut off your living quarters and work on the populace in the back room."

"Oh, shut up!" Christine gave her sign a final blow with the hammer and walked inside. She intended to clean the place now, so that she could move in the following day.

Mirrie came out as she went in, and blushed violently when she saw Allen. She hated to have him see her with Will.

He said absently, "Hello, Mirrie, Will. Stepping out?"

Will said, "Yeah," and Mirrie's flustered voice drowned him out. "He's got his car here—giving me a lift—"

But Allen had already turned away and was walking toward Julia's shop next door.

The interesting people at Julia's cocktail party turned out to be a married couple who were customers of hers, and she eventually maneuvered the foursome out to dinner at a local inn. Allen returned home at a late hour, with a bad taste in his mouth and an irritable realization that he would not be able to do the reading that he had planned. Eating, drinking, smoking, and dancing—oh well, it was probably good for him, only it took up so much time. He'd have to get some sleep. The morning was all too close.

He was thoroughly annoyed to find that he couldn't sleep. He kept thinking of Christine moving in beside him like that, when she very well knew how he felt about women doctors. Her mother had been a doctor, and that was what their quarrel had been about. He'd opened up his mouth and aired his opinions freely. Christine hadn't spoken to him again. She'd gone away, presumably to start studying to be a woman doctor herself.

He laughed a little in the darkness. He wasn't so violent on the subject now. He was older and more tolerant, and he realized that just because one of the breed had done a nasty job on his mother was no reason to condemn them all.

He turned over restlessly, and the bedclothes bunched uncomfortably around him. He *must* get some sleep. What was it he always told his patients? Never feel that you *must* sleep if you can't. Get up, relax, move around, have a glass of warm milk, read the paper, and when you get tired, go back to bed. All right, he'd try it. Might as well see whether it worked. If it did he could give the advice with more authority.

He walked around the room and found that it was a bore. He'd read, then, even though he felt too tired to read. He picked out a book and sat down, and then he got up again. The warm milk—he'd almost forgotten that. He put on a robe and slippers and went out into the hall.

There was always a dim light burning in the hall, and so he saw Agatha quite clearly as she emerged from her room. She wore only her nightgown, a faded cotton print, and her body was more revealed than he had ever seen it before. She had never appeared even in a robe, and he backed into the shadows of his doorway, fearing that he might embarrass her. He watched her walk to the head of the stairs, her hair swinging in two long, heavy braids.

It was as she started down that he realized something was wrong. He could see her face now, and it was blank and without expression. She descended with one hand sliding along the shining banister, and he followed quietly.

He trailed her through the kitchen and into her little sitting room, where she turned on the light, and it was then that he knew she was sleepwalking. She had a box under her arm, and she tossed it carelessly onto a chair, turned away, and left the room. She went upstairs again, and he followed and listened outside her door; but as far as he could make out, she went quietly to bed.

He shook his head a little. He'd have to tell her in the morning and see what he could do about it. Anyway, she seemed quiet now, and he wanted to go to bed himself. He went to his room and then came out again almost immediately. He'd get the milk anyway, even though he didn't want to be bothered with it. He was making a test, wasn't he?

He went down, got milk from the refrigerator, and poured some into a small saucepan. While it was heating, he went into Agatha's sitting room and picked up the box she had thrown onto a chair.

His eyes opened wide as he pried off the lid and stood looking down at a revolver.

Chapter 4

ALLEN closed the box and put it back onto the chair. When he returned to the kitchen, he found that the milk had boiled over, and he burned his fingers pouring it into a glass. He tried to wipe up the mess on the stove, but no matter how hard he worked he couldn't get the burner he had used to look as clean as the others. He left it with a shrug, at last, and went upstairs, but his mind was on the gun. He shouldn't have left it down there. It would have been better to have brought it up and taken it to her, even if he had had to wake her. He didn't want to wake her now, though, but he'd have to talk to her in the morning. She needed treatment. Ought to have brought the gun up, anyway. Oh well, nobody would touch it there.

He tried to read while he drank the milk, but he was so tired by that time that he presently fell into bed and went into a heavy sleep before he could turn over.

He was up at seven, with Agatha still on his mind, and he decided to find her before he had his breakfast. He knew that she arose very early and did some of her endless cleaning before she went down for her coffee, and he presently found her in the rooms she had rented to Christine. She was washing the woodwork.

She turned around with her cleaning cloth suspended. "Good morning, Doctor. I've rented these rooms, and I'm trying to get them ready for my tenant. She's moving in today."

He nodded. "Yes, I know. But these rooms look very clean now, and the movers are simply going to mess it up again. You're wasting your time."

"Oh no. I want to start her off right, you see. She's a doctor, but she says she's going to do her own cleaning, says it will be cheaper for her that way. And as far as I'm concerned, I have enough to do without taking care of this suite."

"You do too much, anyway." He leaned against the wall with his hands in his pockets. "Why don't you get a cleaning woman in once or twice a week? I'm sure you can afford it. There's no mortgage on the house, and you must have a fairly comfortable income from it."

"Do you think I could put up with one of those sloppy creatures? I should say not! They track in more dirt than they clean out. I know them!"

Allen shrugged and reflected that, knowing her as he did, he shouldn't have bothered to bring it up.

"All right, Agatha. It's your problem, but you'll have to figure out some way of taking it easier. I caught you sleepwalking last night."

Agatha's cloth dropped to the floor, and she stooped to pick it up. "Why, Doctor! I'm sure you must have been mistaken—I mean   "

Allen shook his head. "You were sleepwalking and you'll have to do something about it. I'll give you some pills to relax you, but you can't go on taking them forever. You'll have to help yourself. You *must* stop this endless housework and get some rest and relaxation."

The look of horror on Agatha's face silenced him for a moment, and he felt as though he had told her to lay down her life.

"Oh no—no. I couldn't just let the place get *dirty*."

"Well, take a nap when you can, or something. I'll give you

some pills, and I want you to take them."

He went into his office feeling a bit baffled. Something for a psychiatrist, perhaps. She *would* be giving up her life if she gave up the cleaning. It was her greatest enjoyment. He sighed and shook some pills into a bottle. Get her started, anyway, and he'd talk to her some more.

Agatha finished washing the woodwork and then went quickly to her sitting room to find out what she had brought down this time. It was still on the chair, and it frightened her. Why had she done a thing like this? Sometimes it was clothing or something from her bureau drawers. But she hated it when she took the gun down. She *must* stop this sleepwalking. Well, the doctor would help her. He'd give her pills.

She hid the box under the cushion of the chair and went back into the kitchen. In an attempt to be easy and casual she said "Good morning" to Em in an unusually cheerful tone of voice.

Em, fists on hips, looked her up and down. "You feel all right?"

Agatha flushed and turned away as Fred Slupp came through the basement door. He said respectfully, "Good morning, miss," and then cast an appraising eye at Em.

She swung around on him and demanded, "What are you crowdin' up my kitchen for?"

"Keep a civil tongue in your head," he snapped. "It's my breakfast I'm wanting."

Em banged a pot on the stove. "Now ain't that a shame! If I wasn't so busy, I'd bust out cryin', because you got a long time to wait before I get around to dishin' yours out."

Agatha said futilely, "Stop it! Stop it at once!"

Fred spared her a glance, murmured "Beg pardon, miss," and returned his attention to Em. "It's well I know that you'd give me the scraps from the plates, fit only for a dog, if you dared. But I'll have me breakfast now because it's hungry I am and all, and you'll be making it for me without delay."

Em laughed heartily. "Would you look who's talkin'—the poor skinny little runt. You got some swell chance of gettin' your breakfast now, brother, unless you eat them scraps you was talkin' about, which ain't such a bad idea."

Agatha escaped to the dining room, where she found only Allen and Mr. Appely at the table. The doctor made no mention of her sleepwalking, in front of this third party, and she felt dimly grateful. He gave her the bottle of pills and told her to take one after each meal, and before going to bed, for a couple of days.

"Having a little trouble, Miss Agatha?" Mr. Appely inquired courteously.

"No—oh no. Just a—a tonic."

"Ah yes, of course." Mr. Appely nodded. "I really think I should have something of the sort myself—"

He glanced at Allen, who pretended not to have heard. Nothing doing, Allen thought grimly. The fat little chiseler had had all the free advice and pills he was going to get.

Fred Slupp walked silently into the dining room and came to a halt by Mr. Appely's chair, where he cleared his throat. Mr. Appely looked up with a frown, and Agatha cried in a fussed voice, "Fred! What are you doing in here?"

Fred was a bit abashed, but he stood his ground long enough to say, "Sir, you should know that Em calls you a gossiping old washerwoman when your back is turned." He spoke firmly and walked out of the room before the repercussions could break over his head.

What these were Allen never knew, because he was obliged to depart in a hurry. He had no wish to insult Mr. Appely further, but he was unable to keep his face in lines of proper solemnity.

He came across Christine standing near his office, attired in a long robe of some gold-colored material with matching slippers, and smoking a cigarette. He stopped and surveyed her.

"Are you trying to decoy my male patients?"

Christine glanced down at herself. "Oh, this. I came early, properly dressed, but I took a shower and I haven't had time to get back into my clothes. The moving men are due here with my things right now."

"You won't snare any of my female patients in that garment," he told her austerely. "And if one of your moving men absentmindedly drops a bookcase on his toe, which seems likely, you'd better send him in to me."

He disappeared into his office, and Christine moved toward the front door. She had seen, through the glass panel, that her van had just drawn up at the curb.

Agatha was coming down the stairs, and she observed the gold robe with uneasy disapproval. She saw Christine admit the moving men and then retreated to the kitchen in frowning silence. No use saying anything, but it wasn't right for the girl to be wandering around in the hall dressed like that. Actually, it could give her house a bad name. She drew an impatient, sighing breath and went into her sitting room, shutting the door firmly behind her.

Em was surrounded by preparations for the day's meals, and she thought that Agatha was annoyed at the confusion of the kitchen. She raised her voice and said to the closed sitting-room door, "Why don't you stay out of my kitchen if you don't like it, you walleyed, swaybacked old maid?"

"That's no way to talk," a voice said behind her, and she turned around to confront Fred Slupp.

"You got a nerve showin' your prune face here after what you done this mornin', you mean little wart."

"Next time it's likely I'll get me breakfast when I'm wanting it," he said composedly.

"Next time you'll get a bust in the snoot that'll part your ears for good."

Fred ignored her and went to the door of the sitting room, where he rapped smartly.

Agatha thought it was Em with some fresh impertinence, and she flung the door wide with a stony face. She relaxed a little as she saw Fred, and he said earnestly, "Miss Agatha, I'm needing some seeds, and I want to complain about Em, too."

Agatha was unable to reply to this immediately, since Em took the floor and held it stridently. In the end she motioned Fred into the sitting room and closed the door.

"Now, what's the trouble?"

"She's at it again, miss—won't write down what she needs so that I've to keep running to the store for things. Every morning I go, and it's no sooner I'm back at my work than she must have something else. She's got no system, and it's no time for my work I'm getting these days."

Agatha twisted a dustcloth in her hands. "I'll speak to her. She has no right to send you out more than once, or twice on rare occasions. What seeds do you want?"

Em had gone on with her cooking, but she was ready for them. When they came out, she told them a few things, although Fred missed most of them because he hurried out of the kitchen, slamming the door behind him.

"There's no use in your carrying on like that," Agatha said coldly. "You are to stop sending Fred on errands all day long. He may go once, and *only* once."

"You wanna eat your morning eggs without salt? Or drink your coffee without sugar?"

"If you forget anything after Fred has done your marketing, you will have to go for it yourself."

Em had a loud and vulgar reply to this and was still giving it voice when Agatha left the kitchen and mounted the stairs to Mr. Appely's room. She always liked this particular part of her cleaning. Mr. Appely was so neat, nothing out of place, nothing disarranged. Even his bed was hardly disturbed, as though he lay quietly in the center of it all night. That particular phase made no difference in her work, of course. She knew there were sloppy people who made a bed by simply pulling the covers up, but she was not one of these. She always stripped down to the mattress and made her beds *properly*.

Christine was finding a little trouble in settling in. Everything had arrived, even the screens she'd bought, but there seemed to be so much. She'd arranged her medical equipment in the back room all right; but the half waiting room, half living quarters in the front would not assort itself properly.

Em wandered in after a while and suggested lunch in the dining room, but Christine declined. She had decided to save money by making her own sandwiches for lunch, and she might as well stick to it. She was sure of a few patients, at least, old women left over from her mother's practice, and she would fight for more. She dropped her tired body onto a studio couch and pictured Allen staring in amazement at the patients streaming into her waiting room.

Agatha worked through the day as usual and carefully took the pills that the doctor had given her. She swallowed one just before going to bed and then lay staring into the darkness, unable to sleep. It was disturbing, for she usually went to sleep at once, and she felt nervous tonight, as well. Did she hear noises downstairs? The doctor had come in and was quiet, and Mr. Appely had closed his door long ago and presumably gone to bed. She had looked in on Christine at nine o'clock to see whether everything was all right, and the girl had told her she was exhausted and expected to sleep forever. Everything was all right, then, and she was just nervous. It was nonsense.

She went off into an uneasy sleep that was turbulent with dreams. It was so confusing. Her father was always there, and Em, laughing, and then nothing but the darkness of her own room, and she was awake again. She was standing at the foot of her bed, trembling and sweating, and she knew there was something, something downstairs. She had to go down—now—at once.

She put on a robe and crept through the hall and down the stairs. There was a light in the kitchen, and she could see Em in her rocker. Only Em was still—too still—and dark red stained the side of her face.

Chapter 5

AGATHA'S GAZE slid away from the still face and dropped to the folded hands in the lap and then to the motionless feet hanging just off the floor. Em looked almost peaceful, she thought confusedly, if you didn't look at her face. The rocker was Em's favorite chair, and she sat there to prepare her vegetables and to listen to the radio while she waited for something to cook. It had always annoyed Agatha, because she could have been cleaning the kitchen while things were cooking, instead of sitting comfortably in a rocker with all that mess around her.

Silly to be thinking of such things now. She must get help, call the doctor. Em had been hurt. She forced herself to look at the face again and felt nausea stir in her stomach. Em wasn't just hurt. She was dead.

Agatha turned away, twisting her hands together. Something had happened, an accident. Her foot struck some object, and she looked down at the floor.

The gun—the one she had brought down last night in her sleep. She stooped and saw that it was bloodstained, and there was blood on the floor under and around it. She straightened her back without having touched it and took an uncertain step toward Em. The wound had not been caused by a bullet. Em had been hit by the gun, and hit in the right place, too. Agatha knew about that. Her father had told her. He had shown her, once, there were certain places on the head where a hard blow was apt to kill instantly.

She stopped the twisting of her hands and dropped them stiffly at her sides. What was she waiting for? She must get help. The doctor—

She had gone as far as the door when she stopped and came slowly back. She had been walking in her sleep again, and she had that gun down here. She realized that tears were rolling down her cheeks, and she smeared them away with the back of her hand. She *couldn't* have hit Em while she was sleepwalking. Surely that was impossible. Oh, of course it was impossible! But the tears kept running, and she knew that she was not weeping for Em, but for herself. She knew about some of the things she had done in her sleep, moving objects out of place.

25

She was wringing her hands again. Her father had as much as said that she was insane, and perhaps she was. He had been a doctor, he should have known. Who would want to kill Em except herself?

She took another look at the still, dead face. She'd have to go to prison for it and perhaps be put in the electric chair. Well, that was quick. She didn't mind that so much. But if they decided that she was insane and put her in the asylum? She would never be able to stand that. Those institutions were so dirty, filthy. It would be far better if they executed her.

A scream pushed up into her throat, but she closed her mouth firmly. What was the use of that. just to make her feel better for the moment? She'd still have to go to prison or the asylum. Filthy places with filthy people in them. Had she really done this? *Could* she have done it?

Hide her—hide Em so that they would never find her. She was dead. Nothing could help her now, anyway. Only, the funeral— Everyone was entitled to a decent funeral, even Em. Well, she could say a service over the body, herself, and plant a rosebush in memory. Em had loved roses. Surely that would be sufficient.

It was one thing or the other. She could scream, and she yearned toward the utter relief of it, but it would only end in disaster. No. It would be easy enough. That closet under the stairs—there was practically nothing in it—she had never cluttered her closets. It had the dimensions of a small room, and it would be a fitting tomb for Em. After all, Em had never wanted to leave the house. She would rather rest here than cold and alone in some cemetery.

She moved into the hall and went around behind the stairs. The closet was clean, she had done it out only a few days ago, but she went back to the kitchen for a dusting cloth. She wiped the walls and floor quickly, her mind urging her to hurry and her sweating hands more clumsy than usual.

She returned the cloth to its place in the kitchen and realized that she was shaking from head to foot. How could she carry Em all the way to the closet? It wasn't possible. She had neither the strength nor the will, nor could she drag her, because that would not be fitting. Oh, the rocker—she could drag the rocker without disturbing Em at all.

But first she must wash off the blood. She hated this part of it, but she forced herself to do it, and then she smoothed Em's rough, graying hair. Now, get behind the rocker and pull.

It was a hideous journey. The chair made odd, protesting little noises that brought out perspiration all over her body. Never mind. It was in the closet at last, and she set the lock on the door and closed it firmly behind her. Now it could be opened from the inside only, unless someone had a key for the outside. Certainly she did not. Her father had had a key. He'd kept things there and had kept it locked, but she never knew what happened to the key. She fervently hoped that it had been lost forever.

She stood outside the door with her head bowed and said a prayer for Em, and then she said one for herself. She did not hurry over this part of it, but when she had finished she almost ran to the kitchen. So much to be done—the gun first, of course. She handled it gingerly but cleaned it until she could see no more stains, and then she cleaned the floor. She was careful to look for marks that might have been made by the rocker on its trip to the closet, although her eyes were smarting and burning. There was only the light from the kitchen and the dim light from the front hall, but she dared not turn on any more. She lit a series of matches, finally, and drew a quick sigh of thankfulness at her foresight, since she now found the box in which the gun had been kept. She supposed that it must have been pushed out with the chair, and she took it back to the kitchen and carefully replaced the gun within its cardboard depths.

She put the box under her arm and took a last careful look around the kitchen. Everything seemed to be all right, and she turned and went quickly up the stairs.

In the safe haven of her room she examined her dressing robe and found that it had various damp spots on it. She put it into the laundry hamper and, after some hesitation, dropped her nightgown in too, although she could find no stains or even damp spots on it. She slipped into a fresh gown, washed her face and hands in her own little lavatory, and then brushed her hair and rebraided it. She turned out the light and got into bed, and then lay rigid, staring through the darkness at the ceiling until the dawn broke coldly over her pallid face.

It was a relief to get up at last. She worked furiously at her usual tasks and then went to the dining room for breakfast with no appetite in her hollow stomach.

There was no one at the table, but the smell of bacon and coffee from the kitchen sent her hurrying out there with her heart pounding in her throat. The doctor, Mr. Appely, and Fred were seated at the table, comfortably eating a breakfast that had obviously been transported directly from the stove.

"Fred!" Agatha's hand clenched itself tightly onto the collar of her dress. "What—what is this?"

Mr. Appely stood up. "Will you not join us, Miss Agatha? As

you see, we have been fending for ourselves. I assume that Em is ill?"

"Em?" Agatha took a step forward. "I didn't know. Where is she?"

Fred was on his feet and he said respectfully, "She's never come down this morning, miss."

He had a crumb on the corner of his mouth, and Agatha stared at it stupidly until some small portion of her brain warned her to behave naturally. She relaxed the tense hand at her collar, averted her eyes from the crumb, and said quietly, "I'll go up and see what's wrong."

"Perhaps I'd better go with you," Allen suggested.

"No, no." Agatha was already on her way to the stairs. "Finish your breakfast. She may simply have overslept, but in any case I'll find out how she feels and what she needs."

Allen nodded and resumed his breakfast without enthusiasm. Fred had made the coffee and toast, which were awful, and he had cooked the eggs and bacon himself, which were worse, if anything. Mr. Appely had squeezed the orange juice, but Allen had an uncomfortable idea that the stuff tasted of his hands, since they had been sticky and dripping with it.

Agatha was panting by the time she reached Em's room, but she was thankful for the opportunity of looking it over before anyone else. There might be something that she'd need to do—

Em's bed was still made, not neatly, but certainly she had not slept in it the night before. Agatha had to check her restless hands from straightening out the wrinkles and adjusting the crooked spread. Better not to touch it. This was the way Em made a bed, and Em had simply left, without a word to anyone. Agatha did not know why. It was safer not to concoct any stories because you might run into snags.

But if Em had left, she should have taken a suitcase, and there was no suitcase in the room. She'd lived so long in the house and never went anywhere, never did anything but listen to the radio, she'd had no need for a suitcase.

Agatha turned away and went on quick steps to the trunk room. All her trunks and suitcases were standing side by side in neat order, and she picked up a suitcase from the middle of a row. Back in Em's room she packed a few essentials from closet and drawers and wondered confusedly why she was bothering. Everything was so messy. How could anyone possibly tell whether things were missing or not? She returned the suitcase to the trunk room and put it in another line which was back against the wall.

She went once more to Em's room, nagged by a feeling that she was taking too long. She should have been downstairs again by this time. It was odd, though, that Em had not gone to bed last night, and she hadn't undressed, either. She had been wearing one of her old cotton dresses.

Agatha moved across to the wastebasket and began to turn the contents with nervous hands. There might have been a note from someone—her nephew—he often left notes.

Yes, here it was. She smoothed the scrap of paper and read, "Aunt Em, wait up for me. I want to talk to you. I'm working late, but I'll drop by as soon as I can."

Chapter 6

AGATHA crumpled the note and dropped it back into the wastebasket. She'd been up here too long. She must hurry back downstairs.

The three men had finished breakfast, but they were waiting for her, and she tried to compose her face. She had made a nervous mental rehearsal on the way down, and she said carefully, "Em is not in her room. I looked around up there and I could not find her."

Allen and Mr. Appely glanced at each other, and Fred allowed his mouth to sag open a little.

"We'd better find her," Allen said abruptly. "She might have fallen somewhere."

Mr. Appely nodded. "I'll come with you, Doctor. We had better start at once."

"I'll show you," Agatha murmured. She followed them out of the kitchen and threw a few words to Fred over her shoulder about getting back to work. She was too far away to hear his answer, but Fred gave it anyway.

"I'll do no work until she is found."

Agatha followed the two men silently as they made their search. They started on the top floor, and Mr. Appely asked her if Em always made her bed so early in the morning.

"I really could not say," Agatha replied distantly.

They looked in the trunk room but did not notice the space where the suitcase had been, nor did they investigate the contents of the wastebasket. They searched the second floor and the first, missing Christine's rooms. Mr. Appely tried the closet under the stairs, but Allen told him he was sure it had been locked for a long time, and they went on down to the basement. Fred joined them at that point and was still with them when they went to the garage and his own living quarters above it. He told them, a little stiffly, that he'd have cleaned up his place if he'd known that people would be pouring in and all.

Agatha had waited in the kitchen while the final part of the search was going on, and when they returned at last, they suggested to her that Em had probably slipped around to the store or to the mailbox to post a letter.

Agatha twisted her hands together and shook her head. "She never goes to the store, and she never writes a letter. But I've been wondering whether she just decided to leave. I've told her so many times that she could get much more money somewhere else."

"She'd not have left here for that reason," Fred said firmly.

"How do *you* know?" Agatha snapped, and then regretted her temper. She *must* be careful. She waited for them to suggest that she see whether Em had packed any of her things and taken them away, but apparently they never thought of it.

Instead, they sat down for another cup of coffee and told Agatha not to worry. Em would surely turn up soon with a perfectly simple explanation.

"Chances are she's trying to annoy you," Mr. Appely said comfortably. "You know how she is."

Agatha nodded grimly, and Allen swallowed the dregs of his coffee and stood up. "Just to make sure that we haven't overlooked something I'll go to Miss Herser and see whether she knows anything of Em."

Agatha had been eying the frying pan in which a few snarls of blackened bacon were cooling unpleasantly. She said absently, "It's *Doctor* Herser."

"So it is." Allen laughed.

"One is apt to forget," Agatha murmured. "She's so young and pretty."

She wished that they'd all go so that she could make herself some fresh, strong coffee. This stuff was awful, just the sort of thing that a man would slop together.

Mr. Appely and Fred departed, but Allen lingered a moment to ask, "How did you sleep last night?"

"Very well," Agatha said, too quickly. "Very well indeed."

"Good." He nodded. "Take the pills for a few more days and I'll check on you again."

Agatha watched him leave and then turned to the coffeepot. She must have some coffee, strong and hot. As for the pills— well, she knew that those things didn't always work. Sometimes they excited the patient instead of relaxing him, her father had told her. Anyway, she had no intention of taking any more of them.She'd have a couple of aspirins instead. She needed aspirin; her head was aching violently.

Allen straightened his tie and knocked on Christine's door. She opened it almost at once and, after identifying him, gave him a brilliant smile.

"Hello! Do come in for a minute. I can't get this couch into place. You see, I need someone at the other end. You don't mind, do you? I'm sure your patients will appreciate you all the more if you're a little late. It enhances your prestige."

"Never mind the jabber," Allen said, advancing on the couch. "Where do you want it?"

Christine showed him, and he added, "Has Em been in here this morning?"

"Who?"

"Em, the cook."

"No, but I smelled her dinner last night. Miss Bunson should hang onto her."

"I suppose you had a date?"

Christine sighed. "I had a ham sandwich. There was a lot to do here and I—er—didn't want to take any more time."

He gave her a faintly suspicious glance and explained, "You can have your meals here any time you want. Just write your name on the pad in the hall a short time ahead so that Em will know. The food's good and the price is quite reasonable."

"Fine," Christine said sunnily, and was conscious of moisture in her mouth. "I'll surely take advantage of that."

"Why do you want the couch over here?" Allen demanded. "This is no place for it."

"What do you mean? Where else could I put it?"

He looked around the room and said irritably, "You have entirely too much furniture. Where do you expect to put the patients? Miss Agatha isn't going to like it if you try and park them out in the hall."

"Don't be so silly. I haven't arranged anything yet. It'll all go in. Don't worry."

"Don't worry!" he repeated bitterly. "No, of course not. I'm supposed to leave you in this mess and attend to my own business, knowing all the time that you'll be tripping over things and breaking your neck. Come on, for God's sake. I'll straighten this out for you and then I can put my mind on my work."

"There is really no necessity," Christine said coldly, "for you to be so officious."

He had already picked up a table, and he paused to say approvingly, "I see you've taken my advice about using the back room for an office. It will work out far better."

"Ahh, shut up!" She glanced at him and yelled suddenly, "Hey! I want that table beside the studio couch so that I can read at night."

"You can't have it. Here, give me a hand with the couch. We're going to move it again."

She picked up the end obediently but protested, "I don't want it this way. You don't understand. I'm going to put screens up."

"You are not going to put screens up," he said firmly. "They can stand against the wall and look pretty, but that's all. I know an interior decorator, and therefore I know the ropes. This room is right, now, and you will kindly damned well leave it that way. It will force you to make up your bed early in the morning. But if you depended on screens, it would be unmade half the time. Do you think a screen would hide an unmade bed from *any* patient? They'd *have* to take a look. Haven't you had enough ailments to know that a doctor's waiting room would bore the ears off anyone, and that any diversion is manna from heaven?"

"Is this personal experience? I thought you were too conceited to go to any doctor but yourself."

Allen glanced around the room. "I think you're all right now. Just sit down and wait for the patients."

"You don't think I'll get any, of course."

"Of course." He gave her a parting nod. "Don't forget to buy some sort of lousy potted plant for the bay there."

He left, and Christine sat down and surveyed her rooms. Well, everything was in order, and everything in the wrong place, but she wasn't going to change it again. She'd have to clean up a bit and do some dusting, but that was all.

The cleaning took an hour, and when it was finished she looked around with a sense of achievement. She took a shower and dressed and then sat down with one of the magazines from her waiting room, a cup of coffee, and a cigarette.

Her first patient walked in some fifteen minutes later. It was Miss Agatha, and she was pink with embarrassment.

"Miss—er—Dr. Herser—Dr. Gremson tells me that I have been walking in my sleep, and I'm afraid I have. Just downstairs to my sitting room and back, but of course it's worrying. He—Dr. Gremson—gave me some pills, but I—please don't mention it to him—only, they didn't agree with me at all. Now I wonder if you would have something for me, to stop my sleep-walking, you see."

Christine decided rapidly that between Allen and herself ethics were not too important, and she said briskly, "Will you come into my office, Miss Bunson, so that I can give you a physical checkup?"

"Oh no, no." Agatha backed away, looking startled. "I don't need anything like that. It's just that I want something to stop the sleepwalking."

"But I'm sure I could help you more if you'd allow me to examine you."

Agatha knew that this was entirely reasonable, but nothing could have enticed her onto Christine's examining table. She took another backward step and said hurriedly, "Of course I'd prefer a lady doctor for that sort of thing, but it will have to be another time when my duties are not so pressing. All the work to be done— But if you could just give me something for now— there are so many new drugs these days—"

Christine realized the futility of persuasion, and she gazed at Agatha thoughtfully. What had Allen given her that had so disagreed with her? Sleepwalking. Well, she didn't quite like to ask if she might look at his pills. She was not going to be allowed to look at Agatha, so what next?

Agatha began to show signs of restlessness, and Christine grinned at her.

"I could keep you from sleepwalking to any great extent simply by locking you into your bedroom at night and taking the key, but of course it's no solution of your trouble."

Agatha's face brightened, and she drew a little sigh of relief. It would be a solution, she thought, if she were unable to get out of her room. "You can do just that for me. It will be a tremendous relief and a great weight off my mind. Then, sometime when I have caught up with my work, I'll come here for an examination."

Christine had been half joking, and she was surprised at this warm response. She said lamely, "Well, at least you'll know that you won't be roaming at night. How long have you been doing this sleepwalking?"

Agatha guessed that it had been going on for some time, but she had no intention of telling the girl that. She said quickly, "I'm not sure," and added, "You are really settled in here now. It looks very nice."

Christine veered to the changed subject with a mental shrug and asked amiably, "Do you like it?"

"Yes indeed. I think the arrangement is most suitable. It will be charming, once you have it cleaned up."

Since she was unaware of Christine's hour-long labors, she left the room wondering why the girl had looked so astounded. Silly child. Still, she was a doctor, so she must have *some* brains. Anyway, everything was going to be all right. The girl would lock her into her room at night, and that would stop the nocturnal excursions.

She walked around beside the stairs and realized that she was passing Em's tomb. Right beside her, with only a wooden partition to separate them, Em sat, dead, in her rocking chair. Her steps slowed and then stopped, and a spray of perspiration dampened her body.

There was no mistaking that sound. The chair was rocking in there.

Chapter 7

AGATHA stood still as the sound died away and felt moisture between her twisting hands. She remained there for some time in a silence that beat against her ears, and at last made her way slowly to the kitchen and sank heavily into a chair.

Em wasn't dead. She was still living in that dark closet, and someone must go in there and get her out.

She got stiffly out of her chair and went upstairs, all the way to the third floor. She passed the trunk room and went on to a larger room where old and excess furniture was stored and to the bureau which was still packed with her father's things. She went through the drawers methodically, looking for the key to that closet under the stairs. It must be somewhere among his things. She'd have to find it, now, at once. Em must be taken out of there and put to bed—given medical attention.

But what would Em say when she was well enough to talk? Better not think of that. She must be taken out of the closet and given care. It was only decent.

She couldn't find the key. She had searched thoroughly and honestly, and it simply wasn't there. She couldn't ask for help, because then they would know that she had put Em in that place, and anyway, it was nearly time for lunch, and she'd have to prepare the lunch herself today.

She shut the bureau drawers and went out into the hall, closing the door behind her. Perhaps it wouldn't matter if Em stayed in the closet for a while longer. She'd get lunch and then start another search for the key.

She went down to the front hall and looked at the pad. Mirrie, the doctor, Mrs. Rost, and Mr. Appely. The lady doctor was not going to be there, unless she did not know that she had to write her name down if she wanted to eat with them. Agatha went to Christine's door and knocked, and then saw the sign that invited one to "walk in."

Agatha walked in. Christine was in the back room, writing out announcements, and when she heard the door open she thought that it might be a patient. She saw who it was and she carefully kept her face from dropping, and to Agatha's inquiry about lunch she explained that she expected to go out as soon as she had finished with her work.

Agatha returned to the kitchen. She slowed as she passed the door of the closet under the stairs, but there was no sound, and as she went about the preparations for lunch she began to feel a little better. Every pot and pan and dish that she used had to be scoured first, but it was a relief to have them really clean at last. Of course she shouldn't be feeling this lift. She ought to get help for Em—call the doctor—

She went as far as the hall and then stopped. Surely she was being silly. She had seen Em, and Em had been *dead*. She knew what the dead looked like. It must have been the wind rocking that chair. What wind? Oh, it couldn't be wind. The closet was sealed. Imagination, then. She wasn't well, she knew that—she'd been walking in her sleep. She must try to be quiet and relax. Her father had always told her that. A person should learn to relax completely, and it would ease the nervous tension. He had said that she was in particular need of relaxation. He'd nagged her about it.

A voice behind her said gently, "I suppose the pills the doctor gave you were to relax you."

The words seemed a projection of her thoughts, and Agatha spun around with a little gasp. She nodded mutely at Christine, who smiled at her.

"You're as tight as a violin string right now. You should have told the doctor that the pills didn't work. Sometimes they don't, you know. It isn't quite fair to him not to tell him. He could give you something else."

"Oh no." Agatha's lips were as pale as her colorless face. "I don't want to bother him. I'd much rather you helped me. I—I'd prefer a lady doctor. You see, my father was a doctor, and I never liked him to look after me, but of course I couldn't refuse him. Now that you're here, though, I'd like you to help me. When I get a little time, I'll allow you to examine me."

"All right," Christine agreed mildly, "just let me know. In the meantime try and relax all over your body. Take deep, slow breaths and let every bone hang loose, whenever you think of it. Look, may I borrow a cake of soap? I've only a thin wafer, and I don't like to be without. I'll get some later today and return it to you."

Agatha supplied the soap, and Christine left. Let all your bones hang loose? Take deep, slow breaths? Her father had never told her anything like that. He'd merely yelled at her. Relax! Relax! Relax! She hadn't known what he meant, but perhaps she did know now. Suddenly she tensed again. The lunch!

It was ready on time, but it was not one of Em's lunches. The paying guests smiled politely and declared that it was very nice, and privately hoped that Em had not departed for all time.

Julia and Mirrie kept asking questions about Em, and Agatha kept replying, coldly and quietly, that she did not know anything. Allen suggested that she get in touch with Em's nephew immediately, and Mr. Appely agreed that it would be wise.

Agatha observed thinly that she did not know where he lived or worked.

Allen turned to Mirrie. "You know where he works?"

Mirrie was mortified. Why should anyone suppose that she knew where the cook's nephew worked? And that Julia sitting there with a mean little smile on her face and her big ears wagging. She gave a laugh that sounded false and silly even to herself. "Why, I think he works at that store on Main Street. Whenever he comes to see Em, he always insists on taking me home in his car, so that's how I know."

Julia's smile became, in Mirrie's estimation, a trifle meaner. "My dear, he has a crush on you. It's perfectly obvious. He's quite a hunk of man, at that. I think you could do worse."

Allen telephoned to the store on Main Street and left a message, and Will Kroning turned up at about three o'clock. He usually went in by the back door, but there was no response to his ring there, since Agatha was up on the third floor looking for the key again. He waited for a while and then went around to the front and walked in. He stood in the hall for some time, regarding Christine's name plate, and at last he noticed the small sign that said "Walk In." Will shrugged. Why not? He couldn't remember having seen a lady doctor before. Might as well take a gander.

She was sitting with her feet up on the couch, smoking a cigarette and reading one of the magazines, but she jumped up quickly. She really ought to sit in the back room, only she hadn't actually expected anyone as yet.

Will's glance was an automatic and expert appraisal of her youthful curves. He nodded approval and asked easily, "Is this pill-slinging dame busy?"

"I am the doctor."

"No kiddin'!" Will's eyes held honest admiration. Curves *and* a brain.

"Can I help you?"

Will extended a large, muscular hand and put it more or less in her face. It took her a minute or two, but she eventually located a small, healing cut. It was well on the way to recovery, but since he wanted it that way, why shouldn't she bandage it and charge him a fee?

"It don't look like nothing," Will said quickly, "but, see, all my cuts get infected. Somebody told me if I'd only get a doctor on the job, quick, I wouldn' get infected and maybe lose a finger or something someday."

"I see—yes. Will you come into the office, please?"

"Sure, only I don't wanna be long. I got a message about my aunt Em—sez it was important. She's cook here, Aunt Em is. You know her?"

"Not really. Someone was asking if I'd seen her this morning."

The finger was soon bandaged, and Will crossed the hall, whistling softly, and poked his head into Allen's waiting room. He ignored the patients and gave Mirrie a broad smile.

"I just been in to the young lady sawbones across the way. Some babe, huh?"

Mirrie said, "Shh!"

Will lowered his voice to a penetrating whisper. "She fixed me up good and I figger I got a new doctor now. It's gonna be fun to get one of them boils on my neck."

Pink glowed in Mirrie's smooth face, and she rattled some papers on her desk. "Wait for me tonight?" Will asked. "I gotta see Aunt Em. There's something blowin'."

Mirrie gave him a quick nod and slid her eyes around the waiting room. They were all looking at her, of course. Even the ones who held magazines had lowered them quite frankly.

Will retreated to the kitchen and found it empty. He looked around a bit and then went to the back stairs and, cupping his hands, bellowed, "Aunt Em! I'm here!"

Agatha heard him all the way up on the third floor, and a small tray that she had been holding fell clattering from her hands.

It was so awful, somehow, yelling for the dead that way. She picked the tray up and put it away and went flying down the stairs.

Will was pacing the kitchen when she came in, and he asked directly, "What gives? Where's Aunt Em? I hadda take time off to come here. She sick?"

"I don't know." Agatha folded her hands tightly together. "We can't find her, and that's why Dr. Gremson called you. She did not appear this morning, and she is not in her room."

"What?" Will scratched his ear. "Where is she?"

"I've just told you. We don't know."

"Well, yeah, but she's gotta be somewheres."

"I dare say," Agatha murmured coldly.

"You dare say what? Waddya mean by that?"

Agatha was still chilly. "She must be somewhere, of course."

"Sure, but that don't help me much."

Agatha turned to the stove. She had to have some coffee. She'd left some in the pot from lunch because she knew that she'd be wanting it during the afternoon. Everything seemed to be going wrong. She'd done no cleaning all day, and how would she ever catch up with it?

Will said, "We gotta find her."

Agatha turned the gas on under the coffeepot and went to the closet to get a cup and saucer.

"I better look through the house here, huh?"

Agatha swung around and said, "No!" sharply. She added after a moment, "The doctor and Mr. Appely searched the place thoroughly this morning. Em must just have left."

"Left?" Will frowned at her. "You know she wouldn't leave here. She was terrible sot. You'd hadda get a shoehorn to get her outa here."

Agatha nodded. "That's why we phoned you, but there's no other solution. She *must* have left."

Fred Slupp came up from the cellar and stepped into the kitchen, and Agatha tried to ignore him. He said defiantly, "I just wish to know if you've found Em yet."

"Nah." Will looked him over. "Gee, Fred, you must know something about where she's at."

Fred chewed his cud for a few minutes, and then he sighed. "Well, I did be seein' her late last night, and she was fair frightened out of her wits. Said she was scared to go up to her room."

Chapter 8

WILL scratched his thick hair vigorously and stared. "Wadda you mean, Fred—you nuts, or something? I never saw Em scared of anything in my life. Matter of fact, I seen her late last night, and she sure as hell wasn't scared then."

Fred was undisturbed. "I'm telling what I know. She said to me, 'Fred, I'm scared to go up to my room. 'Tis a ghost, for sure, that runs around this place at night.' "

"Nonsense!" Agatha said sharply.

"It's the truth I'm telling you, and I won't be given the lie. She said it was the ghost of the old doctor."

"What old doctor?" Will asked.

Fred indicated Agatha with his elbow. "Her father."

"Absurd!" Agatha's face was darkly flushed. "There is no ghost in this house. Em was trying to frighten you."

"She was kiddin' you," Will said uneasily.

"No."

"At what time did you see her last night?" Agatha asked.

Fred studied the ceiling and after a certain amount of thought said simply, "I don't know."

"Was it before Will came, or after?"

"That I can't tell you. Not a word did she say about him, but said only what I've told you."

"What were you doing in the kitchen at so late an hour?" Agatha asked severely.

"I'd run out of towels, and I came to get some, and there was Em, sitting in her rocker. I got me towels, and she said what I told you."

"Did you notice what time it was when you got back?" Agatha demanded.

"No."

Will took a restless turn about the room. "Look—whatsa difference? We got to find Em. I'm gonna search the house—she must be here somewheres."

"No," Agatha said rigidly.

Will turned on her. "I gotta find her, see? You want I should call the police?"

"No! No, of course not."

"O.K., but I gotta do something. I can't just leave it lay."

"I realize that we must search," Agatha said carefully, "and I shall go with you, since I know the house, but I should prefer that we had someone with us."

Fred cleared his throat, and Agatha swung around quickly. "Not you, Fred. Please go back to your duties."

"All right," Will agreed, "drag some guy away from what he's doin' if you must, but let's get goin'."

Fred returned to the basement in silence, and Agatha wondered wildly what she ought to do next. Get someone—she must point out the missing suitcase this time—someone with a little intelligence. The lady doctor! That was it. She would do very well.

"Come on," she said to Will. "I'll get the doctor."

"He's busy. I just seen his waiting room."

Agatha was already out in the hall. She hoped the girl was there. She'd said something about going out. Will followed, and his bothered frown relaxed into a smile when Agatha knocked on Christine's door. There was no immediate answer, and he explained, "See, you walk right in. It says here on the door."

Christine appeared from the back room with her coat on.

"Oh." Agatha came to a stop. "You are going out?"

"Just to mail my announcements. These are the last, and I want to get them off."

"Hand 'em over, Doc," Will said amiably. "I'll drop 'em down the chute for you."

"I had wanted to ask a favor of you," Agatha put in quickly. She did not want Will to explain things in his crude way, and she went on, "My cook, Em, seems to have disappeared, and although we have searched the house, her nephew wishes to look for himself. Would it be too much to ask you to accompany us?"

Christine was a bit puzzled. She hadn't listened too closely, since her eyes had been on Agatha's white-knuckled, twisting hands, but she said courteously, "Not at all, Miss Bunson. I'll be glad to help."

"Thank you." Agatha turned and led the way out of the room, and Will held the door for Christine with a manner that he had not known was in his repertoire.

"Let's start down here," he suggested, but Agatha was already halfway up the stairs, and they had to follow her. She went straight to the third floor and led the way into Em's room.

"You see that her bed is made, and I am convinced that Em never made her bed before she went down to get breakfast, so I feel sure she didn't sleep in it last night."

"It's like I told you," Will said impatiently. "We oughta look downstairs first."

"We shall get there." Agatha's face was cold and composed. "Now, suppose we look in the other rooms up here."

She showed them the two other attic rooms and led them to the trunk room last. She said nothing of the missing suitcase, but they did not notice it, and as they were about to leave she held them back with a hand on Christine's arm.

"Wait a minute. Look! I believe someone has taken a suitcase."

They turned back and walked over to the empty space, and Christine nodded. "There is one missing. You can see the clean space here, and the marks at the edges."

Agatha flushed and murmured apologetically, "I should never have left the cleaning on this floor to Em. I might have known that she wouldn't keep things right. I don't know what she did with her time, but everything she handled was messy."

"Em worked plenty hard," Will said belligerently. "Wotsa sense keeping a room like this clean, anyways? I guess she did skip, though, but where'd she *go*?"

"We'd better go back to her room and see whether anything is missing," Christine suggested.

They turned away, and Agatha wondered wildly what she had put into the suitcase. She could not remember, and her hands were cold as she pawed through the few shabby garments that still hung in the closet. "Her spring coat is not here," she said at last, "and the—the blue dress is missing. The winter coat is here, but the hat is gone."

"Hat?" Will said, astounded.

"Yes, the hat."

"I never seen Aunt Em in a hat as long as I knew her."

Agatha dusted off her hands. "She went to the store occasionally, and she never bothered with it the. But when she went visiting there was a hat that she wore, a sort of cap with a flower on it."

"Musta ben an old one."

"Oh yes." Agatha closed the closet door. "She hasn't been out much lately, you know, not since you came to town to live."

Will nodded. "Yeah, I know. She always liked me best, Em did. She liked Pa, but when he died, she never came out much no more. She don't think so much of Ma, and she likes me better than Ginny."

"Perhaps you'd better phone your mother," Christine said, "and see whether she's gone out there."

"Yeah, I'll do that. I don't guess we need to look around here any more."

Agatha drew a long, quiet breath. They'd know now that Em had left—, nd everything would settle down.

Christine and Will went out together and accompanied each other as far as the box on the corner, where Will mailed the announcements. He went off then to telephone to his mother, and Christine continued on an idle ramble through the neighborhood.

She came upon a book and greeting-card shop after a while and wandered in. The interior immediately produced a severe-looking woman who asked in a threatening voice if she could be helped.

Christine circled around her and murmured, "No, thanks. I'm just looking."

The woman followed her as she peered through a rack of greeting cards and was still at her elbow when she went on to a careful examination of the books.

"What type of book are you looking for?"

"Nothing in particular," Christine muttered, and wondered if she dared leave.

"If I knew what you wanted, I'm sure I could produce it for you."

Christine picked up a tome, glanced inside, and replaced it. "Well, it's a gift. I'm just trying to get an idea."

"How old is the person?"

"I—er—really don't know."

"You must surely know if this person is elderly or youthful," the woman said.

Christine sighed and murmured, "Elderly."

"Ah! Now, is it a man or a woman?"

"Man."

The woman settled her glasses, thought for a moment, and then nodded. "I have just the thing."

She made for a shelf at the back of the shop, and Christine crept to the door, slipped out, and hurried up the street without looking back.

She went straight home with a faintly guilty feeling that she should not have allowed herself this walk. After all, there just might be a patient, and she ought to be there.

She went into Allen's office, and although there were no patients waiting, his nurse was there.

Mirrie looked up, and jealousy soured her expression. She was jealous of a good many people and had recently added Christine to their number. Trying to make up to the doctor because she was young and pretty, and a doctor, herself. Mirrie had never been able to get any response from him, so why should anyone else?

"Good afternoon. Is the doctor in?"

Mirrie pretended not to recognize this visitor and said briskly, "Not in right now. Do you wish to make an appointment? May I have your name?"

Christine said, "I'm the doctor from across the hall," and was a little taken aback to see a sneer slide across Mirrie's face. She resisted an impulse to pull one of the immaculate gilded curls and added, "I'd like to see the doctor as soon as he comes in. Do you expect him before you leave?"

Mirrie nodded. "I'll give him your message."

"Thank you."

Christine returned to her own rooms and surveyed them with loving eyes. They were beautiful, and the whole setup was perfect.

She went into the hall and wrote her name on the pad. The only other name was Mr. Appely, and, whoever he was, she thought that she wouldn't quarrel with him. She felt wonderful.

Agatha had planned a simple dinner. The cleaning had fallen so far behind that she was anxious to get back to it. If she worked late into the night and speeded things up tomorrow, she might almost catch up.

The kitchen was much cleaner already, but every time she opened a drawer it sickened her. She really must get after them. They were dreadful.

And then she opened the wrong drawer. She knew it, even as she stretched her hand, but she pulled it open, anyway. She remembered now what was in it. Keys. All the keys to the house. Why had she forgotten? Her father had put all the keys in that drawer shortly before he died. They were mixed in with other things, string, rubber bands, a notebook and pencil. The key to the closet under the stairs was in a box of its own away at the back. She remembered it all now, and she pulled the box out with stiff, reluctant hands.

She expelled a long, slow breath as she saw that the box was empty.

Chapter 9

AGATHA looked into the empty box and wondered vaguely why the key was not there. Her father must have taken it out some time before he died and put it somewhere else. But the dust and disorder in the drawer were simply awful. She would have to clean it out thoroughly. There was a round piece of ash from a cigarette lying right in front of the box, too. There was no mistaking it. She had seen that sort of ash. Mostly in ashtrays, of course, but people missed occasionally and dropped the stuff anywhere. On a chair, a table, or the carpet, anywhere. It was infuriating. If she had her way, she'd stop all smoking—such a dirty, unnecessary habit. She wanted badly to clean out the drawer at once, but there was no time. She had to get the dinner, and she must go into the hall first and see how many people were expected.

Three. Mrs. Rost, Mr. Appely, and the lady doctor. She returned to the kitchen and shuddered as she passed the closet under the stairs. So awful to think of Em's dead body in there. But nobody would know. The key was lost, gone, and she had no idea where it was.

She busied herself with preparations for dinner, and as she worked her mind strayed back to the piece of cigarette ash. She didn't smoke herself, and Em didn't smoke. Will Kroning did, though, and it seemed probable that he had dropped the ash, poking around in places which were no concern of his.

Christine saw Allen drive up and come into the house. She heard him go into his office, and she smoothed her hair and settled her dress, but when he came out again, he went upstairs instead of coming to her rooms. She frowned and went out to the hall to call him, but he had already disappeared. She shrugged and decided to wait until he came down.

She missed him again. The next she saw of him, he was getting into his car in front of the house, and he appeared to be freshly washed, brushed, and dressed. Going on a date, probably, and didn't have time to respond to her message. Rude of him—he could at least have told her that he'd see her some other time.

There was a knock on the door, and Mirrie walked in, looking pleased.

"The doctor asked me to tell you that he couldn't see you tonight. He's very late—has a dinner engagement. He said he'd get in touch with you sometime tomorrow."

Christine nodded courteously and closed the door, and Mirrie walked off feeling offended for no particular reason. She returned to Allen's waiting room and busied herself with a few last-minute chores and then changed into her street clothes. Will had not come, and she wasn't going to wait for him—why should she? She titivated overlong at the mirror and tried not to wonder what had happened to him. He'd only gone to phone his family, and he could have done that right here in the house. What did it matter, anyway? She didn't care whether he showed up or not.

He walked in, whistling cheerfully, and said, "Hi, babe. All set?"

Mirrie licked her little finger and ran it carefully over one eyebrow. "Well—"

"Hungry?"

Mirrie attended to the other eyebrow and murmured again, "Well—"

"Come on, kid. I could eat a horse."

"Where were you?" she asked accusingly.

"I went out to phone my folks. Couldn't do it here with all them busybodies pasting their ears against their doors. I phoned a couple friends of Aunt Em's, too, but she ain't ben there."

Mirrie adjusted her hat. "Have your people heard from her?"

"Nah, but they're a ways out in the country. Might be she ain't got there yet."

"Don't say 'ain't.'"

"Ahh, listen, baby. Wadda you care what I say? It's the way I ack that brings in the gravy, and I'm gonna do the right thing by you."

Mirrie was conscious of a little flush of pleasure. He must be in love with her, all right—but, oh, if he were only a little more polished! Maybe she could be a good influence on him, teach him how to speak and behave in front of people like Dr. Gremson and Julia Rost, and that stuck-up piece across the hall. None of her friends need know that he was the nephew of a servant. If only she knew how much money he made! It would be nice to have a house where she could entertain in style. She'd always wanted that.

They went outside, and he handed her into his car. "I'm gonna take you round plenty, babe, and pretty soon you'll find out how's about it. Then when I ask you, you'll know what to answer."

It sounded as though he were hinting a proposal, and she gave him a pale smile and occupied herself with the clasp on her purse.

He started the car and gave an automatic and expert glance over his shoulder before pulling out from the curb. "I seen Aunt Em last night after I took you home, and I told her how I felt. She sez to me, 'Are you sure you know your own mind?'

"I sez, 'Sure I know my own mind. That dish is for me, and all I got to do is work on her. She ain't no cheap slop. She's a dainty lady and she got to have things right, so I need to get a loan from you to buy a house with. Down payment. After I got it I can keep it goin' because I make good wages.' "

Mirrie was impressed, although she winced at the word "wages." He must have noticed when she mentioned once or twice that she'd like someday to have a house. She was pleased, but her voice was prim as she asked, "What did your aunt say?"

"Sez she wants to talk to you. All she seen of you was when you was eating. She told me you eat nice, but she don't know if that's enough."

Mirrie's lips tightened against her teeth, and her eyes became bleak. Interviewed by a servant to find out whether she was good enough for the servant's nephew! The nerve of them!

"So I sez to Aunt Em, 'Sure, she'll come and chat with you. Be glad to.' And now she ain't there for you to chat with."

"I hardly think it matters," Mirrie said coldly.

"Sure it matters. She ain't spent a nickel in so long that they got mold on them. If she lends me the money, she'll have to blow the dust off it first. She's got plenty, and she's gonna leave it all to Ginny and me, anyways, so likely enough, we'd never have to pay it back."

"She's leaving half to Ginny?"

"Yeah. Em's brother was our father. We're her only blood relatives."

"I thought she was married once?"

"She was," Will said easily, "but we ain't heard from the old goat for better than twenty years."

"Suppose he turns up?"

"Why do you want to go lookin' for trouble, baby?" Will patted her arm. "He couldn't get Em's money, anyways."

Mirrie shifted slightly away from him. "How much has she got?"

"More than you ever seen at one time. She bought stocks and bonds, and they went up. She's rich. Not just well heeled, but rich. She never spent nothing, but put it all in securities. She's been doin' like that for years. She's loaded."

Mirrie thought it over for a moment and then reduced the space between them. Will placed one arm around her waist and kept the other skillful hand on the wheel.

Agatha introduced Christine to Julia and Mr. Appely and then took her place at the head of the dinner table. Julia was full of curiosity and asked Christine several questions about who she was and what had brought her to Miss Bunson's. She managed this without seeming to pry, which was a specialty of hers.

Mr. Appely shook his head and said mildly, "It seems a lot of training for a girl, when she will no doubt give it all up and marry someday."

"But I'd never dream of giving it up," Christine protested. "It's much too interesting, and I love it."

"My dear young lady!" Mr. Appely was very much in earnest. "You are really too attractive to remain single all your life."

"Well, I don't want to remain single, but I certainly expect to keep on with my work if I marry."

"I wish you luck," Julia said, rolling her eyes, "but most men are so unreasonable."

Agatha glanced up and seemed to forget about the fork that was halfway to her mouth.

"I deny that," Mr. Appely said spiritedly. "It is always the women who are unreasonable."

Agatha lowered her fork, with the food still on it, and asked, "Who would do the cleaning and look after the children?"

"My husband could see to that part of it," Christine said, laughing.

Julia and Mr. Appely laughed with her, and Agatha smiled because she did not wish to seem ignorant of the joke, but she didn't really understand it. Someone had to do the cleaning and see to the children, and there were cooking and dishes, as well. Actually, it would take three people to do all that. Children always tracked so much dirt into a place, and who could afford two maids these days? Certainly Em had been cheap, but you couldn't tell her anything. Only, she wouldn't have to put up with Em any more. Agatha looked down at her plate and drew back a little. She could not finish the meal.

After dinner Mr. Appely extended a general invitation to come up to his room and watch television. Julia and Christine accepted, but Agatha explained that she was busy.

She was glad that they did not hang around the table, smoking and talking, as sometimes happened. She washed the dishes and noticed with pleasure that they looked much cleaner. No greasy scum on them now.

Fred came up from the basement, and Agatha realized that she had forgotten him, since he usually ate with Em. She went to the refrigerator and began to pull out food with nervous hands. Fred thanked her and sat down at the kitchen table.

"Don't bother with the wash-up, miss. I'll do it myself when I've eaten my food."

"No, no." Agatha was already busy at the sink. "You can dry the dishes for me, if you will, if you really dry them. I don't like my dishes put away wet."

"No more do I." Fred wiped his mouth with a sweeping gesture of his arm. "It's wet they were when Em put them away. Many was the time that I offered to dry them for her, but she would have none of it. I was too slow, and she wanted to get through before Christmas, so she said."

Agatha eyed a dish before placing it carefully on the rack and said, "I suppose Em got tired of working here. I guess she decided to take a trip, or something of that sort."

Fred nodded. "She'd plenty of money for trips, or anything else. And just like her, too, to go off, and never a word to anyone." He picked up a towel and added, "I'll have me piece of pie after drying these for you."

Agatha murmured, "Thanks, Fred. I *do* want to get through here. I've a lot of cleaning to do, what with the upset today."

Fred worked in silence for a while and then asked suddenly, "Where's Em's rocker?"

Agatha had finished with the dishes, and she hung up the damp cloth with exaggerated care. She was on her way out of the kitchen before she replied vaguely, "Rocker? Oh, yes. I saw it somewhere."

She hurried into the hall, but she had not gone far before her brisk steps slowed to a stop.

The door to the closet under the stairs was hanging open.

Chapter 10

AGATHA felt the shock down to the ends of her toes and fingers. She stood perfectly still, with her eyes fastened on the dark aperture, until sharp pain in the palms of her hands caused her to relax the nails that had been biting into them. On a sudden impulse she took two swift steps and shut the door with a small crash. Was it still locked? She pulled at it and drew a long breath. Now it would need the key to open it again—whoever had the key. Or perhaps Em was not dead and had simply walked out. She could open the door from the inside. She might be up in her own room right now.

Agatha started swiftly up the stairs. It would be good to find Em up there, and all this just a nightmare that was behind her. She tried to brush from her mind the basic conviction that Em had been dead when she'd put her in the closet.

Em was not in her room. It looked just the same, and a hasty glance through the closet assured Agatha that it had not been disturbed. She felt tears seeping from the corners of her eyes, and her mind was swept into a rushing waterfall of confusion.

She'd do her cleaning. It was way behind, and it would steady her. She went down to the second floor and started to work with a blind, driving energy.

Julia, seated comfortably in Mr. Appely's room, heard the sound of activity and shook her head. "Can you beat that woman?" she asked Christine. "Never stops her scrubbing from morning until night."

"Who?"

"Agatha. Miss Bunson. Personally, I think she has a hole in the head."

Julia lit another cigarette and stretched back into her chair. She and Christine were having a companionable conversation, since they had been unable to see much in the way of television. Mr. Appely had proved to be the sort of owner who preferred tuning in the set properly to watching the picture.

Julia tried to steer the talk to Dr. Gremson. She had heard that he and Christine knew each other, and she wanted the details, but Christine came back determinedly to Agatha.

"I suppose you know why she concentrates on housework to the exclusion of everything else?"

Julia didn't. "My dear, she's just a bore. I hear you lived over in the hill section. I wonder why we've never met. I've spent a lot of time over there."

"I've been away, studying. Did you know her before her father died?"

"Who?"

Mr. Appely said, "Which would you prefer—a variety show or a quiz program?"

"Whichever you can get in clearly," Julia said amiably.

"Television sets are my big problem, you know. It's very hard to fit them in with the decor."

"Does this Agatha have any friends who come in to see her?" Christine asked. "Does she go out with anyone?"

"Oh, she's just an old bat." Julia dropped ash onto the carpet and then, with a glance at Mr. Appely, rubbed it in with her toe. "She used to go out once in a while with a girlfriend, but since the friend moved away she just stays in the house. A few old friends of her father's used to come in and see her after he died, but they realized that they were just interrupting her work, so they quit."

"All twisted up like a pretzel," Christine murmured. "I wonder how she could be straightened out."

Julia laughed. "Why worry about her? She's probably happier than most of the people you know. She has a tremendous interest, and she loves it."

Christine shook her head. "She's not relaxed. The cleaning drives her. There's something wrong."

"There, now," Mr. Appely said, turning knobs, "that's better, isn't it?"

"That's fine," Julia declared heartily. "Very clear."

Mr. Appely straightened up and turned around. "I saw you in my shop today, Miss Christine."

"Your shop?"

"I was about to come out," he said with gentle reproach, "but you left. Before my clerk could help you."

Christine blushed. "Oh yes, I saw someone outside—friend of mine. Sorry to have missed you."

She and Julia presently departed, declining Mr. Appely's offer of wine and cookies, and went down the stairs together.

"You come on over to my place," Julia said, "and I'll give you something better than cooking sherry and stale biscuits. Not that I'd say a word against Mr. Appely, the old fool, but Agatha's dinners are not like Em's, and I need something to paste together the bits and pieces she handed out tonight."

Christine smiled happily and made no protest. She was hungry, and every little bit helped.

They met Allen at the front door, and Julia hailed him with delight. "We are two lone women, and you are exactly what we need. You must come with us and exhibit your male superiority."

"I've just left a loaded dinner table," he protested. "It and I were both groaning, and the hostess keeping an eye on me to make sure that I wasn't too shy to come back for seconds. I can eat no more tonight, and perhaps for the next week."

"Did I say that we wanted you just to feed you? Christine and I paid good money for a meal that Agatha prepared with one hand while the other clutched a scrubbing brush. We're hungry, even if you aren't. You can have a drink. You look dull, anyway."

"Did you eat like a pig," Christine asked, "and then leave as soon as they stopped feeding you?"

"This one never stops feeding you," Allen said gloomily. "I left at the point of saturation because it seemed the only thing to do."

"Have you been officially introduced to your new competitor?" Julia asked, her eyes darting from one to the other.

"We have met," Allen said gravely.

Christine laughed. "I'm not his competitor yet. I'm thinking of standing out in the hall and trapping his patients as they come in—try to get them to switch over to me."

"I hear you've trapped one of them already." There was a touch of frost in his voice, and Julia gave an audible little gurgle of pleasure.

Christine was chilly too. "I sent you a message, and perhaps one of these days you'll manage a few minutes from all your pressing duties to attend to it. In the meantime, we needn't bore Julia with business matters when she's entertaining us."

"Come on, dears." Julia took an arm of each. "I expect we're dirtying up Agatha's hall with the soles of our shoes."

She walked them out and along to her shop, and when they went upstairs to her office Christine gave a gasp. "Why, this is lovely! How can you call a place of such beauty an office?"

"Oh, my dear, all my business is done in this room. It looks dainty, but as a matter of fact everything is very practical. It's necessary to have it this way. It's my profession, you see."

"Yes." Christine sighed. "My place was fixed up by a blundering amateur. Someday I'll get you in to tell me what's wrong."

"You promised me a drink," Allen said to Julia. "And if you find anything wrong with her place, you will kindly keep it to yourself."

Julia took Christine with her and showed her the compact little kitchenette and the bedroom and bathroom beyond. Christine admired everything, and then was sent in with Allen's drink while Julia prepared their supper.

"While we're alone," Christine said directly, "I'd like to get Agatha off my chest. She came to me and said she wanted help because she was walking in her sleep—said you'd given her some pills which didn't work. I told her she ought to let you know that they hadn't worked, but she wouldn't hear of it—

didn't want to offend you. She said she'd prefer a lady doctor, anyway."

"That's settled, then." He flicked moisture from the bottom of his glass. "You have your first patient."

"I had my first patient when I was working with Mother, and what's more, I still have her. I had a few others too, and I still have them. Today I bagged a new one, the cook's nephew."

"Will Kroning?" Allen stared at her. "What's wrong with the oaf? How can you attend a male patient?"

"You attend female patients, don't you? What about Agatha— that I stole from you?"

"I have plenty of patients," he said crossly, "and I don't care how many you steal. As for Agatha, I've never charged her anything, not even for the damned pills that don't work."

"Why not? She can afford it, can't she? Anyway, if she's mine, and you do seem to be fired from the case, I *shall* charge her. I don't think she'd want to take charity—and I need the money."

Allen took a long swallow from his glass and then gazed down at what was left. "Would it be a breach of anything at all if I were to ask timidly what you propose to do about her unfortunate habit of walking while she's asleep?"

"Well, at least I'll have more time to study her case and get to the root of the trouble."

"And in the meantime?"

"In the meantime, I'll tell her to stop taking your lousy pills, because I have a safe and sure method of keeping her in her room at night."

Allen so far forgot himself as to show interest. "What?"

"I'll lock her in and take the key."

Allen drained his glass and put it down carefully. "I have forgotten, or perhaps I never heard, from which school you graduated. Do they decorate the diplomas with pink roses and blue ribbons?"

Julia came in with a tray and put it down on a low table. "I believe I smell a quarrel—, nd I simply won't have it. We're supposed to be having fun."

Allen glanced at the tray and averted his eyes. "We were talking shop. Not that it sounded much like it. Any doctor listening in would have been a bit puzzled, to say the least."

"Come and eat this while it's hot, Christine." Julia moved dishes and poured coffee with efficient hands. "Now, don't tell me, Allen, that you are one of those stuffy creatures who believe that women should stick to the well-known Home."

Allen denied it with a trace of temper. There were a great

many fields open to women, but he did not think that women were suited to medicine.

"It's pure jealousy," Christine said coldly. "If you show serious competition to a man in anything, even if it's modeling corsets, he'll say that women aren't suited to it."

"Well, darling!" Julia said, laughing. "I don't think you're at *all* suited to modeling corsets. You're too slim to need them."

"Do you know what time it is?" Allen asked abruptly.

Christine glanced over the empty tray and sighed contentedly. "I suppose it's getting late."

"It's nearly midnight. Have you attended to your patient?"

Julia looked up. "What patient?"

Christine got to her feet. "They taught me something of psychology in that pink-floral and blue-ribboned school. I observe my patients, and I know that this one won't be needing me before one o'clock at the earliest. However, I can take a hint, and I shall go."

"Your psychology slipped on this one," Julia told her. "I never get anywhere with him when we're alone. He freezes on me. I make better time when other people are about."

"You could compromise him and make him come up to scratch. He's a babe in arms with old-fashioned ideas, but I don't know whether it's worth it. Good-by, Julia. I've enjoyed myself, and I'm grateful to you."

Christine was almost running by the time she returned to the Bunson house. She *had* forgotten Agatha, and she hoped only that she was right about her still being up.

She was not on the first floor, and Christine started up the stairs. She had gone about halfway when her patient's voice beat against the quiet night in a shrill scream.

Chapter 11

CHRISTINE bounded up the stairs in the general direction of the scream, and Mr. Appely appeared from his room, attired in a neat dark robe. He indicated Agatha's room, and they went in together, without knocking.

Agatha was standing by the bed, fully dressed, with her hands clenched into tight knots by her side. Mr. Appely stayed by the door, and Christine hurried over and eased her to a sitting position on the bed. She tried to get her to lie down, but Agatha whispered agitatedly, "No, no. My shoes—dirty up the blankets. I—I'm sorry to have bothered you. I was taking a nap—nightmare. I had a nightmare."

"I'll go back to my room," Mr. Appely said quietly. "You'll let me know if you want me?"

Christine nodded, and after he had closed the door behind him, she turned to Agatha. "You'd better lie down. I'll take your shoes off."

"No—no, please! I haven't quite finished. I'm almost caught up, but I must finish. It—it was just a nightmare."

"Look, we don't have to tell anyone else." Christine patted her arm. "But you didn't have a nightmare, or a nap, either. You were not lying down, because you have your shoes on, and there's no chair in this room on which you could nap. They're too straight and uncomfortable."

She pushed Agatha back on the pillows and removed her shoes before lifting up her feet. When she appeared to be comfortable, Christine sat down on the bed beside her. She had noticed the scrap of paper that Agatha clutched so firmly in her right hand, but she said merely, "I'm not going to ask you why you screamed."

Agatha's head relaxed onto the pillow, but the knuckles of her right hand were still white. Christine ignored the hand and casually removed a strand of hair that lay across the shiny forehead. "You know, you'll have to stop this incessant cleaning, and you'll have to quit looking in the corners. It's too much for you. The place is hanging around your neck. You should give it up. Couldn't you sell it?"

"Oh no—no."

"Why not?"

Agatha's head moved from side to side on the pillow. "There's Fred, and—and Em."

"What have they to do with it?"

Agatha explained about her father's will, and Christine snorted. "You could get that changed. If there isn't enough to support them, nobody could expect you to maintain them by your own efforts. I'll get you a good lawyer tomorrow. You should get away from here as soon as possible."

Agatha closed her eyes, and when Christine would have started talking again, she raised her left hand in a quick gesture.

"I love this house, and I love the furniture. I'd have nothing to live for if I couldn't keep the house nice, and keep it clean.

Nobody keeps a house in as good condition as mine."

Christine was silent for a moment, her forefinger tapping against her lip. "Perhaps you don't like having to rent out some of the rooms?"

Agatha's eyes opened wide. "Oh, I don't mind that. I'm making my own living, and the house is mine. All mine. Father never allowed me to change anything, but now, of course, I can do as I like. And I like to have a clean house."

"Then what's bothering you?"

Agatha turned her head away. "I don't—this walking in my sleep—I don't like it. It frightens me, and when I wake up, I find that I've moved things out of place. I hate things to be disarranged, and I do it in my sleep."

Christine got up and moved slowly around the room. She knew that Agatha's eyes followed her from under half-closed lids and that Agatha was terrified of something about which she had no intention of speaking. If she could only get hold of that piece of paper which was still clutched so tightly in the rigid hand. Well, there might be an opportunity later. She returned to the bed and sat down again. She'd try something else.

"Tell me about your father."

Agatha shook her head a little. There was nothing to tell, really, and she thought that perhaps she'd better undress now and try to get some sleep.

"Not just yet. What about your father? What was he like?"

Agatha started with a few polite, reluctant words, and then slipped into a steady stream of talk. The other daughter had been the favorite, a gay, disorderly person, and the two of them had sneered at Agatha. They had laughed at her passion for cleanliness and order, and Em had sided with them, without being too open about it. Agatha was inclined to suspect that her father had arranged his will, in regard to Em and Fred, merely to annoy her. Em had done well on the stock market and could easily have retired in comfort. She had vastly more money than Agatha, but she stayed on simply for spite and to continue sneering where Agatha's father and sister had left off. It had been terribly difficult, really infuriating. Em was such a slop, everything messy, nothing really clean. Yet she'd had to pay her a salary when she didn't want or need her.

Christine took another turn about the room, and Agatha's eyes continued to follow her. She returned to the bed again and realized that Agatha was more relaxed, except for the hand that clutched the paper.

"Did your father play golf?"

"Yes."

Christine nodded. "He enjoyed it, just as you enjoy keeping nice furniture in good condition."

"Well, but it's different." Agatha looked a little puzzled. "Golf is a game, and the cleaning is work."

"No." Christine shook her head. "It isn't work, and you know it. It's fun, and you enjoy it, just as your father enjoyed his golf. But he had no right to sneer at your hobby. After all, you have something to show for it, and all he had was a few lost golf balls."

Agatha was interested now. She kept her eyes on Christine's face, and there was something alive and expectant about her.

"What about your sister? I suppose she was a good-time Charlie too."

"Yes—oh yes."

Christine nodded. "I don't know why people look down their noses at other people's interests. I suppose your father and sister were simply jealous because your interests and pleasures were productive rather than just time wasted, like their own."

Agatha drew a long breath, and the knuckles of her right hand receded into the flesh for the first time.

"Your interest in the polishing and cleaning of this house is perfectly normal. It's your house, and you've a right to do as you like with it. But you must take care of your health too. Go to bed on time, don't miss or neglect your meals, and take a walk every nice day. You need some fresh air."

Agatha blinked, and two tears slid out of the corners of her eyes. "You don't know what it means to me to hear you say that. They said such awful things to me. Father used to hint that I— that I wasn't quite right, mentally—"

Christine laughed. "Your father, like so many people, disparaged anyone who didn't think along his own lines. You are more like your mother?"

Agatha raised her head eagerly from the pillow. "Yes. Em told me—Em worked for my mother. I was only eight when she died, but Em said I was just like her, wanting everything just so. I never *could* stand dirt and disorder."

"Of course not. You have your tastes, and they've *yours*. Don't let anyone tell you ever again that your tastes are foolish or abnormal. They're as good as any and better than most. Now, you'd better go to sleep, and you don't need a pill because you've nothing to worry about. I won't lock your door either. You're not going to walk in your sleep again. Em has gone, and if she comes back, we'll get you a lawyer."

Christine was conscious immediately of having made a mistake. Agatha's body stiffened, and the knuckles of the right hand showed white again. She let a moment or two pass and then said easily, "Your father and sister were absolutely wrong, and there's no need for you to walk in your sleep and disarrange things any more."

"No. No, I won't, not ever again. They *were* wrong. You needn't lock the door. I'll be all right. I believe I could sleep now."

"I'll help you to undress."

"No, no, please. I'm quite all right now. You have made me feel a great deal better. I'll go right to bed."

Christine left a little reluctantly. Agatha was not all right, but she'd only upset her by hanging around. Probably she had never undressed in front of anyone in her life.

In the hall, Mr. Appely stepped from the door of his room and whispered, "What was the trouble?"

"Shh. Just nervousness. She's been working too hard."

Mr. Appely nodded seriously and waited to hear more, but Christine said, "Good night," and went on down the stairs. Mr. Appely retired to his room, and presently Christine came up again, very quietly. There was a tall narrow chair, not far from Agatha's door, which stood in the shadows of the dimly lit hall, and Christine hoped that she would not be noticed if she sat in it and remained very still. She could hear Agatha's restless movements behind her closed door.

Agatha still had the piece of paper crumpled in her right hand, and she was wondering how she could have lost her sense of caution so completely as to scream in that stupid way. Still, the lady doctor had helped her. It was satisfying to think of her father playing his silly golf and her sister wasting time with a lot of worthless people. She, herself, could contemplate the lovely glow of old furniture, the shine of crystal and silver, and the faint smell of lavender that came from carefully laundered, exquisite linens. But she must take a walk on fine days. Well, she could do that. She'd make a point of it. She'd buy a few clothes too. She had enough money for that, and perhaps some curtains. She really needed new curtains. It would be hard to force herself to go out, but still—Those two buildings so close to her house, one on each side, rather spoiled it, but it was a fine old house, anyway. She ought to have it painted. Probably there was money enough for that. Father had always kept it painted. All he cared about was show, the look of the outside. She had a pleasant feeling of sneering at him, and she had never done that before. He'd been a doctor, certainly, but had he been such a good one? He'd left hardly anything in the way of money. He'd been jealous of her because her interests were in worthwhile things, and he'd spent his money on himself and his girlfriends. Really disgraceful, with her mother lying in a grave that bore his name.

She fingered the curtains at the window. The house was hers to do with as she pleased, and he was dead. He hadn't known so much, anyway, just a lot of talk and bluster. Oh, she could feel well now, well and happy, andbegin to make plans, if it were not for Em.

Pain streaked across her head, and she pressed the back of her wrist against her forehead. It was just as well that the girl hadn't locked her in. She'd have to go down. Now, or some time during the night. She'd undress and put on her robe, and then if anyone saw her, they'd think she was walking in her sleep.

What was she going to do when she went down? What *could* she do? Horrible! It was all horrible! She'd just finished cleaning her room and had started to take off the spread and turn back the blankets. She hadn't been quite ready for bed, but she'd wanted it prepared for her. She'd moved the pillow, and there was the note.

Perhaps, though, it was good instead of bad. Somebody had written the note, and it might be that this same person had killed Em, and that Agatha had nothing to do with it.

She opened up her hot hand and smoothed out the piece of paper.

"Get me out of here and back into the kitchen. I want a decent funeral. Em."

Chapter 12

DID someone think that she was mentally deranged? Well, she wasn't. Her father had hated her, and he hadn't minded hinting to people that she was not quite right. She had thought, when her sister ran off with that fellow, that her father would turn to her, but instead he'd withdrawn even more, and he'd let others know what he'd thought of her. She felt a sudden fury for him that she had never indulged before, even in her thoughts. She had a right to her own interests, didn't she? The person who had written this note thought she was unbalanced, as her father had hinted, and so hoped to scare her into believing that Em had written it. But Em was beyond writing. She was dead.

Someone else had written the note, then, someone who had a key to that closet, and this person had opened the door, hoping that Em would be discovered. Nobody had discovered her, and Agatha had closed the door again, so the note had been written in an effort to get her to haul Em out.

She wouldn't do it. She couldn't, anyway, because she didn't have the key. Why was it necessary that Em be found? Well, the money, perhaps. Em had a lot of money. That nephew would want her discovered, since he would not be able to get the money otherwise. Oh, that must be it! He had the key. He'd dropped ash in the drawer when he found and took the key, and he had killed Em and left Agatha's gun there so that the thing would be blamed on her. Em must have known that she walked in her sleep and she'd told him, and he'd planned the whole thing along those lines. He must have been frantic when she'd hidden Em. Let him be frantic! Why couldn't he have pulled Em out himself? Perhaps he would do it. Perhaps he was doing it even now. She might go down to the kitchen tomorrow morning and find Em there, sitting in her rocker.

Agatha covered her face with her hands. No—not tomorrow. He'd wait first to see whether she would do it, and probably the door was open right now, to make the gruesome job easier for her. She shuddered and whispered, "I won't do it. I won't."

She was desperately tired and her head ached. She took some aspirin and decided to go to bed at once. Her mind was more at ease, though. She was convinced now that she had not injured Em, and she drifted off to sleep almost immediately.

Christine, still sitting outside, heard her get into bed and sighed with relief. She had begun to think that the restless movements would never cease, and she watched until the line of light beneath the door was blotted out. She settled back into her chair, and when Allen came quietly up the stairs he did not notice her.

"Good night, Doctor."

Allen started and swung around, but it was a moment before he located her in the shadows. "Good God!" he said peevishly. "What are you up to now?"

She stood up and stretched. "Be quiet, will you? My patient has just gone to sleep."

"Oh?" He eyed what he could see of her in the gloom. "I suppose you can see through walls?"

"I can remember what I was taught of psychology. If she was awake, she'd have to be moving around. She's emotionally disturbed."

"They supplied you with dictionaries in that school," he said coldly. "Or perhaps you had to buy your own. Have you locked her in?"

"No. I want her to walk, because I intend to follow her. That way, I may be able to get at the root of her trouble."

"I've tried that already, but the root of her trouble is still buried, as far as I'm concerned. Of course I'm a mere stupid male."

"Not at all. But you can understand that I wish to see for myself."

Allen jammed his hands into his pockets, leaned against the wall, and stared at her. "I'm only a country doctor, and you'll forgive my inadequacies, I'm sure. Will you give me eventually a full report of the case, using words of few syllables?"

"Are you talking the way you would to another male doctor?"

"No."

Christine sighed. "You'll never get over that silly prejudice, will you?"

"Prejudice be damned. You're a young and attractive woman. I thought you were addicted to psychology."

Christine laughed and then glanced anxiously at Agatha's door. "All right. So what have you been doing at Julia's all this time?"

"For one who might possibly be engaged to another, and only you would know, I was misbehaving myself. I kissed her."

"You shouldn't tell."

"I'm not telling. I'm confessing. She's been pressing a sale on me for some time, and tonight I broke down and bought the thing. She was so pleased that she kissed me, and I kissed her back."

Christine giggled. "That's awful."

"What's awful about it?"

"At your age you ought to be able to get a little more kissing out of an attractive woman than that."

"Someday," Allen said carefully, "I shall take your diploma out of its frame and stuff it down your throat, and then give you some little white pills to relieve indigestion."

"It isn't framed. It's still tied up with a blue ribbon. Listen— it's all right to have your fun, but you ought to be married. It's expected of a male doctor."

"Yes, of course, but how can I give my broken heart to any trusting young woman?"

"You're still young," Christine said, regarding him critically, "but your hairline has already receded, which gives you more forehead than you're entitled to have. Patients don't like to be treated by an elderly bachelor."

"My damned hairline is the same as it always was," Allen declared in a furious undertone. "What about your hips?"

"What about them?"

"You never used to have any, and now you waggle them when you walk."

"I do not waggle them," Christine said coldly. "I developed them because I like swimming, and all the suits are made with bulges in those, and other, spots."

Allen gave her an easy smile. "You don't make yourself quite clear. Do your patients always understand you when you tell them to take two after each meal and one before retiring? And isn't it odd that we still can't help quarreling, even after all this time?"

"Go to bed and get some sleep so that you'll know what you're doing tomorrow."

"You'll know what you're doing, even though you sit here all night?"

"Oh well—" Christine shrugged. "I don't expect much in the way of patients tomorrow. I have a tough case here, and I want to crack it."

"Don't come and crow to me when you do. Just remember that I wasn't given enough time on it." He yawned. "You need a cup of strong coffee if you intend to sleep in that chair."

"Thanks for the advice, but I can't leave my post."

"It wasn't advice." He yawned again. "I was talking to myself. I'm going to get it for you."

He went off downstairs, and Christine had to swallow a remark that she had just thought up, because she couldn't call out after him. They had been talking in low voices, and she did not want Agatha to wake up again.

He returned presently with the coffee, and a sandwich wrapped in wax paper. "The coffee is for now, to keep you awake, and the sandwich is for later."

"Do you mind," she asked, "if I eat the whole thing now?"

"Look," he said practically, "I just saw you put down a fancy load at Julia's. What do you think you're doing? You have the hips now, so why not let it go at that?"

Christine took a bite and said absently, "I always eat any food I see in front of me, because who knows when the next meal will turn up?"

"Good God! Are you *that* broke?"

"What?" Christine was still vague. "Thanks very much. That was nice."

"Don't mention it. Would you like a book on psychology, to pass the time?"

"No, thanks. I'm going to sleep now. Not that I want to speed you on your way or anything."

"If you're going to sleep, why did I give you coffee to keep you awake?"

"I don't know, I'm sure." She stretched out in the chair. "Coffee never keeps me awake. It was very good, and I thank you. Good night."

He walked off, and she arranged herself as comfortably as possible and closed her eyes. She slept lightly and awoke once or twice with a pain in her neck. The night had grayed with the coming of dawn when at last she heard sounds in Agatha's room, and she was wide awake and alert in an instant.

Agatha emerged in a dressing robe and slippers and made for the stairs. Christine allowed her to get halfway down before she dared to move, since she had observed that this was no sleepwalking excursion. Agatha was awake.

Christine leaned over the banister and saw that she had gone around beside the stairs in the direction of the kitchen, but she had stopped, and Christine had to stop too. Whatever she was doing, her movements were quiet, and Christine let several moments pass before she crept down the remaining stairs. Agatha was not in sight, and she moved forward cautiously. She did not know the house very well, and they were both startled when she came upon Agatha quite suddenly. She was standing with her hand on the knob of the door that led to the closet under the stairs.

Agatha gave a little cry, and Christine said quickly, "Oh, it's you, Miss Bunson. I thought I heard someone in the hall here, so I came out to investigate." She nodded toward her own door a short distance away.

Agatha had moved back from the closet, and her hands twisted and pulled at the cord of her robe. "You—you woke me up. I must have been sleepwalking again."

"No," Christine said quietly, "you were not asleep this time. You're not going to walk in your sleep again, ever. Don't you remember? You came down on some business of your own, and it's no one's business but yours."

"No, but—"

Christine smiled at her. "I suppose you're going to catch up on your cleaning before the day starts. It's after five. And look at me. I went to sleep in my clothes. I had some studying to do, and my eyes closed up over the book."

"Oh, yes." Agatha's restless hands quieted. "I—I slept very well, but I woke up early, and I remembered, just a few little things that I'd like to get done before breakfast."

"Of course." Christine gave a yawn that ended in a little laugh. "I'll go to bed and try to get a decent sleep. I suppose you'll be getting dressed now and starting your work."

"Yes. Oh yes." Agatha drew a long breath. "It will give me a good start, and I've had a nice sleep. I don't need any more."

They parted at the foot of the stairs, and Christine went to her own rooms. She waited until she was sure that Agatha had disappeared, and then she emerged again and crept to the door of the closet under the stairs. She turned the knob, but it seemed to be locked.

She was suddenly conscious, with a stiffening of her back and a prickling of the hair on her scalp, that someone had opened the kitchen door behind her and was watching her.

Chapter 13

CHRISTINE turned quickly, but the kitchen door was closed and there was no one in sight. She hesitated for a moment and then forced herself to walk to the door and open it. The kitchen was gray with the dawn, but there was no other light, and it was deserted. She wondered uneasily who would be up at this hour and decided that it might have been the odd-job man, Fred something-or-other. Perhaps his day started early.

She returned to the hall and went up the stairs and to Agatha's door. There were sounds of quiet movement in the room, and she supposed that Agatha was dressing in preparation for a long day of cleaning. It seemed that there was nothing more to be done now, and she might as well go on down and get some sleep. She went back to her rooms, undressed and got into bed, and then crawled out again to lock the door. It wouldn't do to have patients walk in and find the doctor asleep in bed.

Agatha was feeling much better as she moved around her room, making herself neat for the day. She was convinced now that someone else had killed Em. She might have known that she would never do a thing like that, even in her sleep. It was a pity that she'd gone downstairs and let the girl catch her like that, but she'd felt that she simply had to see whether the writer of the note had left the closet door open for her, and he hadn't. It had been closed and locked. She intended to find out who this person was, and she was in a good position to do it—she was around the house all day. She was strongly suspicious of Will Kroning, because surely Em's money was at the bottom of this thing, and who else would benefit? Well, the sister, of course, but she hadn't been around the house, and it seemed very unlikely that she'd had anything to do with it.

Agatha got so much cleaning done before breakfast that she decided to get up earlier every morning. She seemed to have so much more energy at this time of the day, and perhaps she'd be able to get around to reading some of her books in the evening.

When she came to the kitchen, at last, in good time to prepare breakfast, she found Fred Slupp there, filling a pail with water.

"Good morning, Miss Agatha. It's little sleep you had last night, I'm thinking. Not once did I get up through the hours but there was a light burning in here. I'd be supposing you'd left it on by mistake but that it was off when I came in this morning."

Agatha turned to stare at him. "Do you mean the kitchen light, or a—a flashlight moving around?"

"I mean the kitchen light, of course. If I'd seen a flashlight I'd say so."

"But—"

"Is Em back, then?"

"No."

"Good." Fred nodded composedly. "You and I can do very well without her, miss. It's plenty help I'll give you, and without grumbling, either. It's likely Em has gone somewhere else, for that one had an eye on the money at all times. It's often she talked of her investments and how clever she'd been with them, and the whole thing just luck, if the truth be told."

Agatha nodded vigorously. "People who have been lucky with money will always tell you that they got rich because they were shrewd and clever."

Fred went down to the cellar, and Agatha turned the gas low under the coffee percolator, with her mind almost at peace. The case against Will Kroning was strong, so strong that she was, herself, convinced.

And then she remembered something, and in her agitation she allowed the bacon to burn. Will Kroning smoked cigars. She had never seen him with a cigarette, and that piece of ash in the drawer had never come from a cigar. Will had not dropped the ash, and so he had not stolen the key.

She carried the breakfast to the table and saw that the doctor and Mr. Appely were supplied. Her own appetite was poor and her mind in confusion. Was a little piece of ash so conclusive, after all, though? Anyone could have dropped it in the drawer, looking for anything, and Will could still have taken the key.

"You seem very pensive, Miss Agatha," Mr. Appely suggested.

"Oh no." She fingered the handle of her cup. "I—I'm never very bright until I've had my coffee in the morning."

"We're all dull," Allen said vaguely.

Mr. Appely offered, by the way of excuse, that he had had a restless night, and Agatha contributed the information that she had slept well. Allen grunted and muttered that they could always talk about the weather.

Mr. Appely considered this a sneer at his conversational powers and gave his attention exclusively to Agatha.

"Has there been any word of Em?"

"No."

"What about the nephew?" Allen asked. "Has he called up about it?"

"No," Agatha said again.

"I'll get Mirrie to phone his place of business today and inquire."

"She ought to know," Agatha said thinly. "I saw her going out with him last night. That's all he cares, out with his girl on pleasure when his aunt is missing."

"Does she go with him often?" Allen asked. "I understood that he merely takes her home."

"Home!" Agatha sniffed delicately. "He takes her out stepping, as Em always called it. Using all his money for drink and dancing and greasy food. He had to borrow from Em every now and then, but of course he always paid it back. Em would never have given it to him otherwise."

"You mean I may be going to lose a good office nurse?" Allen said, smiling at her. "But perhaps she'll keep on with her job after she's married."

"Oh, they're not engaged." Agatha made a little face. "They just go out. I don't think Mirrie wants to marry him. She's just passing the time. She has grand ideas, and she wants to live well when she marries. Everything will have to be good, nothing cheap. Will doesn't have that kind of money."

"Unless—" Mr. Appely began prosily, and Allen finished, "Unless something has happened to Em, and he inherits."

Agatha paled and dropped her eyes to her plate. That was it, of course. He couldn't inherit anything until Em's body was found, and so he had sent her the note. Trying to frighten her into pulling the body out again, and he hadn't left the door open for her.

Allen and Mr. Appely had lighted cigarettes, and Agatha watched them with an impatience that she tried to conceal. So many people smoked cigarettes. Why should Will Kroning be an exception? Why did he prefer those horrid cigars? But perhaps he took a cigarette occasionally. She'd never seen him with one, certainly, only that didn't prove anything. He'd said something once—what was it? That cigarettes were corny. And what did that mean exactly?

Agatha washed the dishes and tidied the kitchen with Fred's help. He was a careful worker, and clean, and she got on well with him. When they had finished, she gave him the list for the day's marketing, and after he had left she went to the front hall. There was a lot to do there, and she was anxious to start.

Christine was awakened by the sound of Agatha washing down the outside of her door. She did not know what it was at first, and she scrambled out of bed and struggled into a robe. She had her hand on the knob of the door before she realized that it was just Agatha and her cleaning, and she shrugged and went to put some coffee in her electric percolator. She was still sipping when a man arrived to install her telephone, which reminded her that she had sent out her announcements without a phone number on them, and of course the number would not be in the directory for some time. She sighed for her misplaced efficiency and realized that she'd have to follow the announcements with supplementary cards.

The telephone did not take long, and she finished her breakfast in a bit of a hurry. She'd better get dressed and tidy up. She'd had two unexpected patients yesterday, and there might be more. She moved swiftly about the cleaning, took a quick shower, and dressed. When she had finished, she saw that it was eleven o'clock and shook her head a little. She'd have to do better than that, get some sort of a system. She'd get up at six and have everything ready for possible patients by nine. Patients? Would she *ever* get any?

Her third unexpected patient walked in before the thought had left her mind.

It was Allen, and he explained, with the utmost gravity, that he had a little time and had decided to use it to get a checkup.

"What do you mean, checkup? Did you come here to see whether I'd rearranged the furniture again?"

"I'm surprised," Allen said, "to find you so lacking in a knowledge of office etiquette, but I suppose it's your inexperience. You should say, with quiet dignity, 'Will you come into my office, Dr. Gremson?' "

Christine eyed him suspiciously. "Why should I invite you

into my office, so that you can chew my ear off about what a menace I am to the human race?"

"There'd hardly be time enough. When I get through telling you about all the mysterious pains I have here and there, you'll naturally want to thump and prod to find out what causes them, and it would be next to impossible to insult you while you are looking at my tonsils."

"Your what?"

"Tonsils."

"You mean you want a *physical* checkup?"

"What else could I mean when I come into a doctor's office and ask for a checkup?"

She looked him up and down for a moment and then said, "Certainly. Come into my office and remove your coat, shirt, and undershirt, if any. You can leave your tie around your neck if you're one of the modest kind."

He followed her in, but before he removed his coat he rearranged the desk and a couple of chairs. "You must have the patient sitting in the light. Your face, no matter how beautiful, should be in the shadow."

"Oh, shut up!" she said, dropping into her chair. "What did you really come here for? A cocktail before lunch?"

"Certainly not. I never drink before dinnertime. Er—aren't you going to drape me with a sheet?"

"I'll take you from the waist up," Christine said coldly, "and leave the rest for the specialists. Now stop jabbering until I tell you to say 'Ah.' "

She wrote her findings down on a neat file card and, when she had finished at last, said, "All right, you can put your things on now, unless you want to leave that undershirt, and I'll give it to Miss Bunson for a cleaning cloth. Actually, you seem to be in very good condition, except for one ear which is slightly cauliflower. A minor operation would fix it."

Allen ran to the mirror and declared in a voice of outrage, "It's nothing of the kind. It sticks out slightly because I slept on it more than the other when I was a child, and I'll have no operation done on it, minor or otherwise."

"Up to you," Christine said carelessly. "If you don't mind looking like one side of a loving cup, I'm sure it'll be no menace to your health. You might try tipping your hat a little to that side."

"I never wear a hat."

"Really?" She eyed his hair critically. "It must be economy, not vanity. That'll be ten dollars, please."

"What!"

"Ten dollars."

"You can't charge ten dollars for an office visit when you're just starting out!"

"That's a special fee for patients who are obviously on a tour of inspection. You wouldn't know about it, but it's a necessity for a woman doctor."

Allen cleared his throat but found no words. He extracted a ten-dollar bill from his wallet, realized that he was overdue in his own office, and hurried across the hall, missing Agatha and a pail of water by a hair.

She stopped in horror as the water nearly slopped over onto the shining floor, and then moved on again with a sigh of relief. She passed beside the stairs, and as she approached the closet under them her breath was suddenly drawn in a low gasp, and this time water splashed jerkily over the edge of the pail and dripped down around her feet.

Fred Slupp had the door of the closet open and was walking in.

Chapter 14

AGATHA cried, "Fred!" and her pail clattered to the floor with a splashing rush of water.

Fred backed out of the closet and turned a startled face. "What is it? What's the matter?"

Agatha did not heed the water that was spreading over her beautifully waxed floor. She swallowed twice before she was able to ask in a whisper, "What are you doing in there?"

"It's my slips, Miss Agatha. I've put them in here for rooting, since it's darkness they'll be needing for a while."

She remembered then. He'd done the same thing last year. He was really wonderful with plants, and although she'd hated having the messy pots in the house, she had allowed it. She drew a quick, sharp breath and asked, "How did you get in? Was the door locked?"

"Yes, miss, it was locked, so I went and got the key in the drawer there."

"Oh, yes." Agatha nodded. But Fred did not smoke, and she added, "Did you put the key back?"

Fred twisted a lock of his hair and muttered, "It's absent-minded I'm getting, for sure. When I found the door locked just now, I looked in me pocket and behold, there was the key, though I'm a one for putting things back where they belong."

"You found the door locked just now?"

"That I did, though I'd left the door open when I put the pots in yesterday, because it's air they need the same as you and me. And didn't someone close it on me when I was off about my business, and so the lock caught and I'd to use the key again."

"I see—yes." Agatha found that her breath was coming more easily. "But you'll have to get the pots out of there, Fred. I can't have them kept in that closet."

Fred's face set like cement, and he replied simply, "No, miss, I'll not disturb them now. They've not rooted yet and must stay where they are."

"Then give me the key," Agatha said rather helplessly. "I'll let you in when you have to look at the things, but I'll keep the key."

Fred surrendered it reluctantly. "I want to be having a look at them now, though."

"No, no, not now. Look at all this water on the floor. You'll have to help me clean it up, and I'm late with the lunch. I need help with that too. You can look at the plants later."

She walked past him and shut the closet door firmly and then slipped the key into her pocket. She was conscious of a cool surge of relief. Surely this explained the note. The wretched murderer who had ended Em's life did *not* have the key and had supposed that she had it. Well, she had it now, and Em would stay in the closet until it was discovered who had killed her. Will Kroning would surely be back this afternoon, and she'd talk to him. She'd find out a few things.

But the lunch was pressing her, and she must hurry. She knew that her meals had not been as good as Em's, although the pots and dishes were much cleaner, but she had decided to try and make the food more tasty. She gave Fred some potatoes to peel and hurried out to the hall to see who was expected. Mr. Appely was bringing a friend again. Annoying, but it could not be helped. Never mind. She had one thing to be thankful for, anyway. The key to the closet was lying in her pocket. She was the only one who could get in there now, unless someone broke down the door.

At the height of the luncheon preparations Will Kroning walked in and asked whether Em had turned up. Agatha said, "No," shortly, and Will scratched his head and decided that he'd better stay for lunch, since he was allowed only an hour.

"Well, I really don't know. I suppose you could sit down here with Fred," Agatha said doubtfully.

"Not me." Will was smoothing his hair in front of the mirror over the sink. "I got money to pay for what I eat, and I'm gonna sit with Mirrie and them others."

Agatha was exasperated, but she did not like to refuse him and at last gave a grudging assent.

Will said, "I'll sit next to Mirrie, huh?"

Agatha shrugged and refrained from telling him that she didn't care where he sat. She wanted to talk to him, but there was no time while she was so rushed with the lunch.

Mirrie was astounded and dismayed to find Will sitting beside her at the luncheon table. She tried to ignore him and made desperate efforts to strike up a conversation with Mr. Appely's friend, who was young and shy, but Will made it impossible by talking long and loud. In the end the conversation was completely dominated by Will and Julia, and Mirrie was almost jealous as they laughed and joked heartily together. On the other hand, she could not help feeling somewhat appeased by the fact that Julia bothered with him at all.

Will ended a loud burst of laughter by looking at his wrist watch and starting suddenly to his feet. "Gee-zuz! I gotta pick up my feet or the boss'll boot my fanny outa that joint." He leaned over Mirrie and said softly, "I'll be back later, baby. Wait for me."

He departed in a hurry, and Julia leaned back in her chair and laughed. "Such excellent material, so crudely finished."

Mirrie blushed hotly, and Allen said to her, "Have you finished? I have some work for you."

She had to go, but she felt that her lunch had been ruined. She'd had no chance to sound out Mr. Appely's friend, and that Julia was nothing but a nasty, long-clawed cat. Still, money was always a big help, and it looked as though Will might be coming into plenty. She could have a nice house and invite Julia over— show her a thing or two. Only, Julia would sneer at the furniture and decorations. She knew all about that sort of thing. Well, she'd fool her. She'd go to a department store and consult the interior decorator, have everything just right.

She worked hard that afternoon because the doctor had evening office hours, and she had to clean things up as she went along. She glanced out of the front windows now and then, and at one point she received a nasty shock. Will was out there with another man and a policeman! She thought he had been arrested.

They came into the house, and Mirrie opened the waiting-room door slightly and peered out. She saw them go through to the kitchen, but there was nothing to appease her curiosity, and she returned reluctantly to her desk.

Will had been responding to a sense of decency when he took his companions to the kitchen. It would not be right, he felt, to maybe frighten the doctor's patients away by the sight of a couple of cops giving the joint a gander. He pulled up chairs for them and then went to the back stairs and called loudly to Agatha.

Agatha was furious because Will's voice always seemed, somehow, to dirty up her walls, and she came running down the stairs. She was terrified when she saw the policeman, but he merely gave her an incurious glance, and it was the other man who did all the talking.

Will introduced them with a flourish. "This here is Miss Bunson—Inspector Lewis."

Agatha nodded mutely, and the inspector said, "I understand your cook is missing?"

Agatha's hands twisted together, but she said quietly enough, "Yes. I suppose she decided to go off somewhere else."

The inspector eased his weight from one foot to the other. He suffered from flat feet but was anxious to keep his affliction a secret. "I believe that a suitcase and a few clothes are missing?"

Agatha nodded, and the knuckles showed white on her twisting hands.

Inspector Lewis's eyes wandered around the kitchen and returned to Agatha's face. "Her nephew is worried because he can't seem to locate her. Would you permit me to search her room to see whether I could pick up any clue as to her whereabouts?"

Agatha's face took on a hunted expression. "But I haven't had a chance to clean up there yet. It's dirty, really disgraceful. I'll get to it as soon as I can."

"No, no," Lewis said hastily, "it's important that I search before you clean. I'm glad to hear that it's still as she left it. May I go up?"

"But I—I'd very much prefer to clean the place first."

Lewis shifted back to the other foot and wondered why she didn't want him up there. Maybe she was just one of these fussy dames who have to spew guest towels around before you can use the bathroom, and then get mad if you so much as move them an inch, much less use them. On the other hand, maybe she had another reason. He'd put it all down in his little notebook as soon as he got a chance. He had only recently been promoted to his present position, and he was enthusiastic to the point of being a sore trial to the accompanying policeman.

Agatha was obliged at last to let him go upstairs. She knew

that it would look bad if she persisted in her refusal, but she had begun to be badly worried about her fingerprints. It was natural that they would be in Em's bedroom, but they must be on the supposedly missing suitcase as well—and what if that were found? She'd have to try to find an opportunity to wipe it carefully.

She followed the men upstairs, although Will tried to get her to stay where she was. He knew the way, he said, and could show them. Agatha, with her mind on the suitcase, hardly heard him.

There was no opportunity to get to the trunk room. The inspector went into Em's room, and Will and the policeman stood in the doorway, blocking her view, but she knew that they'd hear her if she left the hall. She paced up and down for a while and then found that the suspense was too much for her. She set her jaw and went back to her cleaning.

Lewis eventually got to the note in the wastebasket and questioned Will at length about it. Finally he asked, "But how much money did this aunt have, that she could afford to lend you enough to put down on a house?"

"Ahh, plenty," Will sighed. "She never spent nothing, see—put all her money in stocks and bonds and things."

"Things?"

"Yeah. Well, like I said. Stocks and bonds and things."

"Just stocks and bonds, or other things?"

"How in hell should I know?" Will said, beginning to get peevish. "She never sent me no printed notice about where she kept her moola."

"Where did she keep it?"

"What?"

"The stocks and bonds, and things. Did she keep them in a bank?"

"Nah. She never went near the banks. Always said them places was run by a lot of pirates."

"What did she do, buy her investments with cash?"

"She never told me, and I didn't ast."

"Did she show you her investments at any time?"

"No."

"How do you know she had them?"

Will stared. "Why, she told me. She often told me things she bought, only, I forget what, now. She told me every time she got money from them too. It always made her feel good, that did."

"What would she do with the dividends? How did she cash them?"

"I don't know."

"Did you ever cash any for her?"

"No."

Lewis nodded and gave Will a glance that was compounded of scorn and pity. He did not believe that any cook would be loaded to that point, and he was convinced that she'd merely been talking to make herself seem important. He moved toward the door and said, "Let me see that room where the suitcase is missing."

Will showed him the trunk room and the empty space, and the inspector looked around in silence. Trunks and bags lined up neatly and in order, and there was no doubt that one had been moved recently. So the woman had just picked up and left. That was all there was to it. Only, he must make sure he hadn't overlooked anything here. He asked to be taken back to Miss Bunson.

Agatha arose from her knees in the upstairs hall as they came down from the attic. Lewis said, "Miss Bunson, could you tell me where your cook kept all her securities? Her nephew tells me that she never used a bank."

Agatha nodded, mopping at her wet hands. "That's right."

"Then where did she keep them?"

"The last I heard," Agatha said dryly, "she was looking for them. She'd change the hiding place once a week, but she forgot where she had put them, a few weeks ago, and she was searching around trying to remember."

Will made an explosive sound with a suddenly released breath. "I'll be damned! I ben a dumb cluck! I thought she was talkin' about one a them lousy soap operas. I wasn't listening good because I was tryin' to pick out a decent apple from the dish. I heard her, though. She sez, 'I found them, all right. The ghost moved them for me before that dirty scum looked there, or I woulda ben robbed of everything.' "

Chapter 15

AGATHA'S SODDEN FINGERS began to make little pleats in the skirt of her dress. This was the second time she'd heard of Em having mentioned a ghost, and she realized now what it was. Em had seen her walking in her sleep, not too close, perhaps, and in darkness, and in her superstitious ignorance had thought it was a ghost. It was odd, Agatha thought, that she would move Em's securities in her sleep, but she must have done it.

"A ghost," Lewis said flatly. "Maybe this Em was a bit off in the head."

Will denied it hotly, and Lewis turned to Agatha, who said that as far as she knew, Em's head was all right.

"Do you know what she meant when she talked about a ghost?"

A direct lie always made Agatha uncomfortable, and her hands twisted together for a moment before she said, "No."

"Do you know who she meant when she referred to the dirty scum who tried to rob her?"

Agatha said "no" again, but without hesitation this time, and Lewis noticed the difference. He made no comment but turned to Will and asked him the same questions.

Will replied with simplicity that he didn't know what the hell Aunt Em had been talking about. He never paid too much attention when she was on her ear. She often sounded off about people trying to do the dirty on her.

Lewis returned his attention to Agatha. "Could you tell me how the woman bought her stocks and bonds and cashed her dividends without using a bank?"

"Oh yes." Agatha was quite easy now. "She used my checking account. I'd write out a check for her, and she'd give me the cash. She'd endorse the checks that she received, and I'd bank them and give her the cash. It was a great deal of trouble and I always disliked it, but she would have it that way."

"Do you think that she kept much cash in the house?"

Agatha nodded. "She usually had a lot hidden around the place, but every now and then she would buy something and clean herself out a little."

"How much cash?"

"Well—" Agatha thought it over. "It used to be several hundred dollars, and then she'd buy something and cut herself down to perhaps a hundred, something like that. She had all kinds of little things, packets and packets of them. Back in the thirties I believe she was in a bad way, but in the forties she was really rich. I think she sold some of what she had. She had not bought much lately, so I suppose she had a lot of cash."

"Why didn't she buy much lately?"

"I really don't know."

Lewis nodded. "Well, since she was afraid of a ghost, and someone more substantial who was out to rob her, it seems probable that she simply decided to slip away. There's the missing suitcase, and a few of her clothes gone too. We'll put out an alarm and try to locate her for you."

Agatha's smile was bright and effortless, and she took the trouble to escort him to the front door.

Lewis noticed this, too, and carefully wrote it all down in his notebook as he stood on the porch.

Will had come out with him and asked, "Wotcha doin'?"

"Nothing."

"That's the police force for you," Will said bitterly. "We got to pay taxes for you guys to stand around and do nothing."

"Sure." Lewis closed his notebook. "If you want better service, why don't you pay more money? Look at this suit. When do you suppose I'll be able to buy a new one?"

"You want me to pull down my hair and cry?" Will demanded. "Who cares when you get a new suit, even if that one shines in the seat of the pants? Which it does."

Lewis had just caught sight of Mirrie peering through the lace curtains of Allen's waiting room. He asked abstractedly, "He a good doctor?"

"Who, Gremson?" Will nodded. "Sure."

Lewis sent the policeman back to the car and went into the house. "I have a little trouble. Guess I'll go and see him."

"He can't see you now," Will protested. "You gotta make an appointment. He's high class. Go on out and phone, and maybe he'll take you next week."

Lewis ignored him and walked into the waiting room, seeking the blonde whose flyaway curls had appeared at the window. He did not notice the desk immediately, but found himself confronted by a bunch of deadpan women and one man, and they were all looking at him. It occurred to him fleetingly that this might be the way to make the fortune he had always dreamed of—entertain people waiting in doctors' offices.

"May I help you?" Mirrie asked.

He turned quickly and saw the desk, well decorated with the blonde. Pretty as a picture with all those curls, and natural, too. Or were they? No use jumping to conclusions. The dames knew how to make curls, and color them as well, these days.

"Any chance of seeing the doctor this afternoon?"

"I'm afraid not," Mirrie said and gave him a sweet smile.

"O.K. I'll make an appointment for tomorrow morning."

"I'm sorry, but tomorrow—"

"Look," Lewis said earnestly, "can't you get me in? I'm in pain."

A voice behind them said grimly, "Why don't you go across the hall? You can get an appointment there right away."

They both looked up to find Will scowling at them. Lewis became conscious immediately that he was leaning too far over Mirrie's desk, and he straightened up. "Across the hall? I didn't notice. I want a good doctor, though."

"This one is tops," Will said emphatically. "I ben treated there already, and the fee ain't high, either. Now this here guy charges too much, and he don't do a thing more for you."

"Please!" Mirrie's voice was an outraged whisper.

"I'll try across the hall," Lewis decided. He gave Mirrie a companionable grin. "I'll be back later and tell you how I made out."

"What for?" Will demanded. "You think she cares how you make out?"

Mirrie was running a sharply pointed pencil over the appointment book. "If it's an emergency, I can manage to fit you in this afternoon."

"No, no, really not necessary," Lewis said, and wondered why women dolled themselves up in colored evening dresses when they looked so much better in a plain white uniform. "I'll see you later."

He departed, and Will muttered, "Get a load of that guy! Comin' back to see you later! Not if I still got my health, he won't."

Mirrie said, "Shh!" and kept her eyes on the appointment book, but she was both pleased and excited. Two men practically fighting over her.

Lewis walked into Christine's waiting room, as the sign on the door directed. No nurse here, and no waiting patients. Either this guy was a bum or playing in hard luck.

Christine was in the office, writing out the follow-up notices of her telephone number. She heard Lewis come in, and after a quick smoothing of her hair and dress she went out to the waiting room. He looked her over and decided that this was a good-looking nurse too, only she ought to be in uniform.

"May I see the doctor?"

"I am the doctor."

Lewis forgot to close his mouth, and after a moment she asked impatiently, "Didn't you see my sign outside? Christine is a feminine name."

Lewis recovered himself and gave her a respectful smile. "I'm sorry. I was across the hall, but he has no time for me today, and someone suggested that I come here."

"I see. I've only just moved in, you know, and haven't entirely established myself."

Lewis was a bit disappointed. The dame probably didn't know much if she'd just started in, but on the other hand, she *was* a dame, and perhaps she could be persuaded to gossip.

"Do you wish to consult me professionally?"

"Why, yes. It's about my feet. They're very painful if I'm on them for any length of time."

"Will you come into the office?" Christine said happily. "And take off your shoes and socks."

Lewis followed her and explained, "I'm a police inspector, and it's a vital part of my business to have my feet in good working order." He sat down and untied his shoes. "Matter of fact, I've just finished this case here."

"What case here?"

"Don't you know?" Lewis stripped off his socks. "The cook is missing, and her nephew reported it—wants her found."

"Oh, yes. Have you found out where she is?"

"Well—" Lewis wiggled his toes. "There's a suitcase missing, and a few clothes, so I suppose she just took off for some reason. Seems she kept securities and cash around the house, and she had indicated that she was afraid someone was trying to rob her. She also mentioned a ghost once or twice."

Christine was examining his feet, and her careful hands became still for a moment, then she said merely, "Oh?"

Lewis noticed the hesitation and asked quickly, "You know something about this ghost?"

"No, what?"

He gave her a glance of unwilling respect. "I mean, have you heard anything about it around here?"

"I don't believe in ghosts."

"Nor do I. So I'd like you to tell me why this Em thought there was one."

Christine had abandoned his feet and was examining his shoes. "These are right for your flat feet. Did you come here to check

on a previous opinion? Because I thoroughly agree with whoever gave it."

Lewis pulled on his socks and said easily, "I don't know
whether you'd call it checking or not. I came here because my
feet still ache."

"You should stay off them as much as possible, of course, but
I'd suggest an orthopedist."

"Thank you." Lewis tied his shoes and stood up. "What is the
fee?" She told him, and as he paid her he asked, "Now, who is
this ghost?"

Christine eyed him. "Are you going to put the fee you just
paid me on your expense account?"

Lewis hoped that the blush that heated his face was entirely
internal. He said, "Look, Doctor. A woman is missing, and I'm
trying to find her. You know something about this ghost, and I
think it's your duty to tell me what it is."

Christine observed the toes of her shoes for a moment and
then sighed. "Yes, I suppose so, if you put it that way. Miss
Bunson walks in her sleep, and the cook must have seen her at
night in the dark and thought she was a ghost. Miss Bunson has
been upset about her condition and has consulted me, so I wish
you wouldn't say anything about it unless you have to."

"Certainly not." Lewis realized that he had left a wrinkle in
the foot of his right sock, but decided that it would spoil his
dignity if he rearranged it just then. "Does anyone else know
that Miss Bunson walks in her sleep?"

"Yes. Dr. Gremson, across the hall."

Lewis nodded, thanked her, and went out. He walked straight
across the hall, and did not see Agatha flatten herself against the
door of the closet under the stairs.

She had decided to remove Fred's plants, and the sound of
footsteps had disturbed her. She did not see who it was, but
when she heard the door of Allen's waiting room close, she in-
serted the key into the lock with shaking fingers.

She was disturbed again when the lady doctor came out and
wrote her name down on the pad for dinner. Christine had decided that these unexpected fees warranted a little extravagance,
and she hoped, although dimly, that Agatha would come up with
a steak. She wrote with a flourish and then returned to her office
and went on with her telephone numbers.

Agatha was breathing heavily by this time, and the key clattered against the lock. The plants must come out, now, she was
afraid to do it at night. Somebody would be expecting her to
pull Em out again.

The pots were close to the door, and she took them out, one

by one, with sweating hands. She had brought a flashlight because she knew that if she left so much as one plant, Fred would miss it and raise a fuss. She hated to throw any light into the depths of the dark, hideous place, but she need not point the flash to the rear where the rocker stood. She'd keep it down on the floor to the front.

She put her thumb on the button cautiously, and the shaft of light showed her that the plants were all out—and then, compulsively, against her will, her wrist swung up and the light streamed over the chair at the back.

The flashlight dropped from her hand and rolled noisily on the floor, and her teeth bit painfully into her arm.

The rocking chair was empty.

Chapter 16

THE flashlight had rolled against Agatha's shoe, and after a moment she picked it up, backed out of the closet, and slammed the door. She leaned against it, her mind frightened and confused. Em wasn't dead. She was lurking in there, somewhere. Agatha pressed the entire length of her body against the door, as though to hold it against pressure from the inside. Oh, if only the door could be locked from the outside, but her father had seen to that. He'd had if fixed so that it would always be possible to get out. He'd said that it would be dangerous any other way. It was a sealed closet, and the air could very soon be exhausted.

She drew away a little, with her forehead puckered. If the closet was airtight, then Em *couldn't* be living, not after all this time. Unless she had walked out long ago. Perhaps she had. She might be upstairs somewhere.

No. Agatha brushed the back of a bent wrist across her forehead and stooped to pick up one of the plants. She put the flashlight away and carried all the plants to the kitchen, and then called to Fred.

He appeared with an inquiring look on his face, and she indicated the pots. It had occurred to her that they had an unpleasant odor, but it seemed to be dissipating.

"You had better take these to the cellar, Fred. That closet in the hall is sealed, and they wouldn't get any air."

"I know that, miss." He was annoyed, though still respectful. "But I left the door open, and somebody closed it. People should leave things alone."

"Take them down to the cellar," Agatha said sharply. "It's where they belong, anyway."

Fred obeyed, but his face wore a mutinous expression of contempt for a world that would not understand the needs of growing things. He observed, more to himself than anyone else, that he would like to be allowed freedom to make a good garden, just once.

When he had removed the final pot at last, Agatha stood in the kitchen and pressed her cold hands against her hot face. She could not even remember what she had intended to clean next. She put a light under the coffee percolator and dropped into a chair beside the table. The cleaning would have to wait while she figured out some course of action. She must think. She could no longer push this thing to the back of her mind and pretend that everything was all right. She had done wrong, very wrong, in hiding Em's body that way. Why hadn't she had confidence in herself? Even though she had been walking in her sleep and had done some peculiar things, she would never murder. Oh, never, never! Sleep might release some things that were repressed in you—but a murderer was something apart.

The door opened behind her, and she turned quickly to confront Julia Rost.

"Found Em yet?"

"No," Agatha said quietly.

"Oh." Julia tapped a brightly polished fingernail against her lip. "I was thinking of having dinner here tonight—but if Em isn't back—"

Fred had returned to the kitchen, and he gave Julia a look of mild surprise. "I don't know why you'd be hankering for Em's cooking, which always turned the stomach in me. It was her dirty hands I seemed to be tasting in all her dishes."

Agatha said sharply, "That will do, Fred!"

"The hands on her were dirty at all times," Fred went on, warming to his theme. "She'd never be wasting the time to wash them, and it was only in the dishwater that some of the muck was soaked away."

Julia sent an involuntary glance at Fred's hands, and found them surprisingly clean.

Agatha said again, "That will do, Fred."

"No." Fred's voice was deeply earnest. "You should be knowing the truth. Em's dishwater was as dirty as the hands on her.

She scraped nothing from the plates before throwing them in, and never a sign of a rag did she pass over them, but picked them out of the water and dried them with a sorry-looking towel. So it's one of her hands was always less dirty than the other, though so slimed with grease that there wasn't much choice at all."

Agatha advanced on him with such an ominous face that he backed away and disappeared in the direction of the cellar.

Julia looked at her own two carefully tended hands and swallowed. Agatha was leaning against the sink with her eyes closed. She had never supervised Em at her work. Em would never have permitted it. But it *couldn't* have been that bad, and she was furious with Fred for shaming her like this in front of the Rost woman.

Christine walked into the room, glanced from one to the other, and asked, "What on earth's the matter?"

Agatha opened her eyes, and Julia swallowed again and gave a little laugh. "Double nausea, just for the moment."

"Fred was here," Agatha said angrily, "telling silly, unpleasant tales."

"I doubt whether Fred has enough imagination to have made that one up," Julia muttered, and shuddered.

"Mrs. Rost! Please—"

Julia shook herself, laughed, and patted Agatha on the shoulder. "Now, don't worry about it. Just forget it. After this I'll eat here only when you are doing the cooking. No one could say that your dishes taste of dirty hands, anyway, though it's funny how delicious Em's dirt could be at times—"

"You will have to excuse me. I have things to do," Agatha said coldly and walked out of the room with her chin up.

"I wanted to talk to her," Christine said, and looked at Julia. "What's all this about Em's dirt?"

"It's better forgotten, my dear. Look, the coffee's boiling. Suppose we have a cup. We can leave a quarter on the table to pay for it."

Christine shook her head. "That's warmed-up stuff. I'll make you some coffee in my rooms. I want you to see my place, anyway, and give me some free advice about the arrangement of furniture."

"But of course." Julia linked arms with her. "I want some free medical advice about my stiff neck, so it will work out very nicely."

They went on to Christine's apartment. They did little talking about Christine's furniture or Julia's stiff neck, for Julia plunged into an account of Agatha and the people connected with her, while Christine listened with absorbed attention.

Julia wound up her recital at last by saying accusingly, "I swear I think you got me in here just to steer me onto Agatha. What do you care about her anyway?"

Christine denied it. "But I *am* interested. She's my patient and I want to know her background, and she's not very communicative about herself."

"Well—" Julia glanced at her watch. "I really must go. I have an appointment."

Christine went to the door with her and invited her to come back later for cocktails before dinner.

"My dear, I'd love it. I'll hurry and get back early."

Christine went out shortly afterward to a local liquor store. She spent the fee she had collected from Allen that morning, and since that reminded her of him, she decided to ask him in for a cocktail too. Better not leave the message with that blonde fluff this time, though. She returned to her office and picked up her newly installed phone.

Mirrie's voice trilled into her ear, and she asked to speak to Dr. Gremson.

"Who is calling, please?"

Christine considered it. No use identifying herself, or the blonde would tell her that Allen would phone back. "I'm his aunt," she said austerely.

Mirrie was surprised, but the voice impressed her. She connected with Allen and said, "Your aunt, Doctor."

"My what?"

"Your aunt," Christine said, still using an accent. "I am across the hall in Dr. Herser's office. Will you come over for cocktails as soon as you are free?"

"I—yes, of course. Is this Aunt Lizz?"

"See you later," Christine murmured, and hung up.

Mirrie had listened carefully, and now she knew all about it. Really, what some women would do to try to make a man! Well, there was no need for herself to go to such lengths, not that she ever would. She had two men after her, and practically snarling at each other. She gave her head a little toss. That Lewis, now—he'd come back and asked her to have dinner with him, and already Will had told her to wait for him. She would have informed him, if he'd given her a chance, that the doctor had evening office hours, and they were both eating with Miss Agatha. There just wasn't time to go out anywhere. She'd told Lewis, and he'd gone right out to the hall and put his name down on the pad. She hoped Agatha wouldn't refuse to accept him. Maybe she could say he was a friend of hers. It would be disappointing if he forgot all about it and didn't show up again.

Lewis had no intention of forgetting. He was on the third floor, after having hesitated wistfully on the second. He wanted badly to go into the various bedrooms, but he knew it wouldn't do. He simply couldn't afford to get caught. So he went on up to the attic to look around until it was time for dinner. It might help him to sit down and have a meal with these people, maybe get a line on what was going on in the place. That Miss Bunson, for instance. She was a queer one. When he'd come out of the doctor's waiting room to write his name down on the pad in the hall, he had seen her walking into the kitchen, carrying some flowerpots. He'd followed her to the door, our she hadn't heard him, and he'd gone away again since he had nothing in particular to say to her. But on the floor he'd noticed a trail of spilled water that led straight to the door of a closet under the stairs. The pots had been wet, then—somebody trying to grow something and keeping them dark and wet until they rooted. The closet door had been locked, with a good firm lock, too, not the ordinary thing that almost any key would open. You'd have to have the one that belonged to it. What valuables did she keep there that she had it locked up so securely? He'd like to get in just to see whether that woman's securities were there. Oh well, probably he was making too much of it. The cook hadn't been gone for long, and these people usually turned up within a day or two. It was only because Will had come around kicking up such a stink that they'd done anything about it today.

He knew Will, They'd been in grammar school together. But Will was still a hick, while he himself had acquired a little polish. He flicked a speck from his sleeve and looked idly out of the window of the trunk room. A good-looking dish with red hair was emerging from the place next door, and he watched her until she disappeared from view. He was bored after that, and he sat down on a trunk and fished a cigarette from his pocket.

Julia did not know that she had been admired from an attic window of Agatha's house, but she was always prepared for anything and liked to be elegant even when she was entirely alone. She went first to Allen's waiting room, and asked Mirrie in a low voice to tell Dr. Gremson that she was in Dr. Herser's office and would he drop in before he went to dinner.

Mirrie nodded and then curled her lip at the smartly draped departing back. No mention of herself dropping in, although Julia knew perfectly well that she always stayed here to dinner when the doctor had evening office hours. Of course an older woman would naturally try to avoid young and pretty competition, and it was really pathetic to see both those females running after the same man. As for herself, she didn't have to raise a finger. She had two men running after *her*. She patted her curls and heaved a small sigh. If only Will were not so—so *ordinary*. That other one was more of a gentleman. Anyway, those cats would see him eating with *her* tonight.

Julia and Christine enjoyed themselves thoroughly over their cocktails before Allen arrived, late, for one swift one.

"What's all this aunt business?" he demanded immediately. "I knew you weren't Aunt Lizz. She always bawls me out before she even says 'hello.' "

"Oh, turn it off," Christine said, fishing for the olive at the bottom of her drink. "I merely wanted to get my message straight to you, instead of relaying it through that bit of lipstick and peroxide you call a nurse."

"She is a most capable—"

"Do shut up," Julia said amiably. "Are you so dense that you don't realize we are merely jealous?"

He looked warily from one to the other. "I'm not going to get caught in the company of you two again."

"It won't be long," Christine assured him. "We are going to pull straws for you, and the one who loses will go quietly."

"Can't you," he asked rather helplessly, "just allow me to go quietly?"

Julia said, "Not a chance," and was interrupted by a timid knock on the door.

Mr. Appely entered, and Christine was immediately conscious of a faint sense of guilt. She should have asked him in for a cocktail, after he had entertained her so courteously with his television. She stood up and said hastily, "I'll get you a drink—"

Mr. Appely raised his hand. "No, no. Really. I was sent in to tell you that dinner is past ready. You must come in at once."

Julia glanced at her wrist watch and made a little face. "I'm afraid we did forget the time."

Mr. Appely turned to Allen. "I have my regular check for Em here. Do you think I should give it to the nephew?"

Chapter 17

ALLEN looked at Mr. Appely and asked in a puzzled voice, "What was that?"

"It is Em's interest check."

"What do you mean? Was it in a letter?"

Mr. Appely was a little affronted. "No, no, certainly not—I should not dream of opening letters not directed to myself. It is the interest on a sum of money that Em loaned me when I expanded last year.

Allen murmured, "Oh, I didn't know that," and rattled some loose change in his pocket.

"It is not a subject that one brings up in idle conversation," Mr. Appely said, still a bit offended. "She offered the money and I accepted, a perfectly reasonable and legal business transaction."

"Yes, yes, of course," Allen agreed hastily. "I was a little surprised, that's all."

"Come on," Julia said in a bored voice. "Let's go."

They went to the dining room where they found Mirrie, every gilded curl in place, sitting between Will and Inspector Lewis. Agatha was in her chair at the head of the table and looked as though she were feeling depressed. As a matter of fact, she disliked Lewis being there and had hinted to him that it was not her custom to serve meals to people from outside, but he had come in anyway, bland and courteous.

Mirrie's small mouth was twisted into a pleased smirk, and she received Lewis's polite attentions, with her little fingers extended elegantly. Will was unusually quiet, and his brows were drawn down over smoldering eyes.

As the others came in Lewis rose to his feet and stood until the ladies were seated, while Will slumped a little farther down onto his spine. Mirrie gave him a scornful flick of her eyes, but he ignored her and announced in a loud voice that they were all late, and what gave with them, anyways?

Agatha introduced Lewis to Julia, Christine, and Allen, and Lewis stood up again. He bowed to the ladies and said that he had already had the pleasure, as far as Christine was concerned.

Christine smiled at him. "Perhaps you can help Mr. Appely.

He wants to know what to do with the interest check he has for Em."

Will's eyes widened. "Whatsat?"

Lewis was just as interested but reminded himself not to be so crude. "Well—" He rubbed his chin. "Hold onto it for a day or so. I don't suppose it's very much?"

"Not too much," Mr. Appely said primly. "She loaned me three thousand dollars."

Lewis glanced at Agatha, and she nodded. "Em sold some of her stocks last summer, things that had taken a sharp rise during the last war. Some of them had doubled and tripled—she'd bought them all in the hundreds. I remember that I had to bring her home quite a few thousands in cash."

"Did she give you the three thousand in cash?" Lewis asked Mr. Appely.

Mr. Appely disliked his personal affairs being brought into the open this way, and he replied shortly, "Yes."

Lewis returned his attention to Agatha. "Was it more than three thousand you brought home to her last summer?"

"Oh yes." Agatha leaned back in her chair. "Several times I brought back some thousands to her. I told her she ought to leave her money invested where it had done so well, but she simply could not resist taking the profit and poring over it."

Mr. Appely said firmly, "I believe it's going to rain tonight, and we need it so badly too."

Will moved restlessly in his chair. "What in hell did she do with all them thousands? I didn't get none of it." He directed a dark look at Mr. Appely. "You sure she only give you three grand?"

Mr. Appely colored to the roots of his thinning hair and rose to his feet. "I resent that, sir. I have said three thousand, and that was the exact sum. She asked that the interest be paid every six months, and today is the due date. The check is in my wallet, made out to her for the correct amount."

"I'm sure Will meant no offense," Lewis said soothingly.

"Wotcha gettin' so hot about?" Will demanded. "I only ast."

"Suppose we eat in peace," Julia suggested. "You can all go out into the garden afterward and fight it out."

An uneasy silence descended and was broken by Mirrie, who began to make gay little remarks to Will and Lewis in turn. She was anxious to keep them both, at this point, and she wanted Julia and Christine to see their devotion to her. Lewis responded most satisfactorily, but Will had his eyes in slits and merely looked at her. However, when he had finished his food, he draped his arm across the back of her chair and leaned toward her. Let

Lewis see which way the wind blew—no lousy cop was going to get his girl away from him, even if he did get up off his can every time a dame walked into the room.

Agatha's eyes darted constantly from one to the other, and as soon as the last mouthful had been eaten she rose to her feet. Her hands were twisted together again, but she said quietly enough, "Good night, everyone."

Christine followed her as she made for the kitchen. "I'd like to have a word with you, Miss Bunson."

As soon as they had gone, Will scowled around at the table. "Get a loada her, willya? We ain't even got time to finish chewin' our cud, and we gotta get out. Just so we got the last crumb in our yaps, we gotta swaller it while we're doin' a lock step for the door. And after we get through thankin' her for doin' us all these favors, we gotta pay a good steep price for it."

Julia grinned at him. "Let's sit around here for a while and fool her."

"Not me." Will stood up and swung his chair back. "Next time she comes in she'll bring a broom with her. I was havin' a cuppa coffee in the kitchen once, and when I go to put the cup back in the saucer, the damn saucer ain't there. I look around, and here's the old bat washin' it at the sink already. That's the kinda dame would make your bed while you're still in it if you wasn't up by six o'clock. No wonder my poor old aunt lifted up her feet and hit the highway."

"There's just one thing," Lewis said, "that makes me think your aunt did not lift up her feet and hit the highway, as you put it."

Will swung around on him. "As I put it. And how would you put it? And who the hell do you think you are—except that I know already. You're Stinky Lewis. I'm real put out that I can't remember your first name—I'm blushin' for myself—but none of us kids in school knew it because everybody called you Stinky from the time you was brought into kindergarten needin' a handkerchief and not havin' one."

Lewis pursed his lips and nodded his head gravely. "Yes, I see. I suppose that's why I took such pains, as I grew up, to acquire culture and polish, and control of childish tempers."

Will knew that he had lost that round, and fury boiled up in him. He pulled Mirrie's chair back from the table, with Mirrie still in it, and muttered, "Come on, baby, let's get outa here." He turned to glare at Lewis and added, "Get busy and find my aunt, Stinky. If you think she wouldn't have left because of all her checks and things, you maybe better hunt for a kidnaper. Some guy who was after her loose cash, see. If she only gave Appely here three thousand, there must be a lot more around somewheres. So get goin' on your big hoofs and earn your pay. Come on, Mirrie. Let's go out and unload some dough."

"Please, Will!" Mirrie got out of the chair and straightened her uniform with nervous little tugs. "I have to work tonight. I've told you before. I should be getting back right now."

"Take your time, Mirrie," Allen said easily. "It's early." It was not particularly early, but he was afraid that Will might accompany her back to the waiting room.

"Sure, you got time. We'll take a spin somewheres so I can cool off."

Mirrie did not want this at all. She had hoped that Will would go and give her a little time with Lewis, but Allen thwarted her again.

"Go ahead, Mirrie. Do you good. You've been working hard. You could take half an hour, anyway."

Mirrie tried to resist, but Allen and Will were too much for her, and they got her out without paying any attention to her bleatings. Allen knew that she did not want to go but assumed a bluff heartiness until she was well on her way.

He went back inside and found Julia and Lewis in the front hall. Lewis was asking if she had known that Em had so much money.

"Dear heaven!" Julia moaned. "If I'd known, I'd have borrowed from her long ago."

"Come into my office for a few minutes, will you?" Allen said. "I had no idea that Will had got the police in on this. I assumed he'd found Em at home, that she'd had a scrap with Agatha."

They followed him, sat down in the waiting room, and lit cigarettes. Lewis dropped his match carefully into an ashtray and said, "It looks as though she'd left. There's a suitcase missing, and some clothes."

"Really?" Julia raised her eyebrows. "But the thing is simply fantastic. Em lived between the kitchen and her bedroom. It was her whole world. If she'd had a scrap with Agatha she'd have stayed and fought it out, and probably enjoyed every minute of it."

Allen nodded. "They had a good many fights, but I never saw Em worsted."

"Perhaps Miss Bunson fired her," Lewis suggested.

Allen explained about the will, and Julia added, "I think the whole thing is utterly absurd. Surely Agatha could have had that set aside, since her father left her no money for carrying out his instructions."

Allen shrugged. "Matter for a lawyer."

"I don't suppose she's even consulted one. You know Agatha's rigid sense of duty. She'd take care of those two until the end of time because it had been her father's wish."

Lewis had been listening carefully, and when Allen asked what he intended to do next, he said, "Well, we have an alarm out for her, but I'd like to search this house from attic to cellar. Could you get Miss Bunson to give me permission?"

"We've already searched the place."

"I'd like to do it myself, though. In fact, it's necessary."

"Why? If her clothes are missing, and a suitcase, it seems obvious that she's left."

"No. He's right." Julia tapped ash from her cigarette, but it missed the tray and fell onto the carpet. "I don't care what's missing. I simply cannot see Em walking out of this house."

"Perhaps you would ask Miss Bunson if I may search the house," Lewis said.

Julia made a laughing little sound of negation. "Not me. She really dislikes me."

"I'll ask her," Allen said, "although I don't like to get her upset. She's not particularly well—been sleepwalking, and she's very tense."

Lewis nodded. "I've noticed. But isn't there some way to get her permission? I don't want to delay on this."

Allen looked at him for a moment in silence. "Aren't you being very energetic for no particular reason?"

"No, I assure you. But I can't search the house unless she allows it."

Allen rested his elbows on his knees and looked down at his folded hands. "I'm probably being very dense, and annoying too, about the thing, but I still can't see it. The suitcase is missing and some of Em's clothes, but why get Agatha all steamed up, when it seems probable that Em will be found tomorrow, or even tonight?"

Lewis stood up and walked slowly to the window, where he peered out, apparently looking at nothing.

Julia glanced at the delicate little watch on her wrist, and crushed out her cigarette in such haste that it continued to smoke. "I must go. I've an appointment."

Lewis escorted her to the porch, and she paused and said in a low voice, "Why don't you search the place during the night?"

"I'm afraid I couldn't do that."

"Why not? I expect Christine could get permission from Agatha for you, for tomorrow or the next day so that she'd have time to get used to the idea, and then we could put her to bed with a pill to blot her out. Tell everyone else about it, and you can search freely, without her around to bother you."

Lewis gazed at her for a moment in silent admiration, and then he said, "Thanks," and disappeared into the house.

He went straight back to Allen and said directly, "Dr. Gremson, Mrs.—er—the Julia one has just suggested a plan to get Miss Bunson's permission for a search of the house at some unspecified time and then to give her something that will keep her asleep while I do the job tonight. I'll need your cooperation, and I believe you'll give it when I tell you that the missing suitcase, with the cook's clothes, is standing up in the attic right now."

Chapter 18

ALLEN said sharply, "What!" and Lewis nodded.

"I'd like it kept quiet, for a while at least. I was up in the attic just before dinner, and I saw a suitcase with a wedge of clothing sticking out at the end. I had looked into some of the cases and trunks, and they were all neatly empty, so that this struck me as being out of line. I opened it and found a few loose garments that could very well belong to the cook."

Allen stared at the floor for a moment and then asked, "Did the suitcase fit into that space, where one was missing?"

"It fitted exactly."

"Well—" Allen drew a long breath. "We should get Agatha to identify the clothing. She's the only one who could tell whether the things belong to Em."

Lewis frowned and shook his head. "No. Miss Bunson is bothered and upset. She probably knows all about it, but I don't want her in on this. I'd like to search the house without her knowledge or interference."

"You're making too much of the thing." Allen rumpled his hair. "How could Agatha know anything about it? She's a decent sort."

"Yes, of course." Lewis paused and added, "But I want to search the entire house carefully, and I don't want her around."

"What are you looking for?"

"The cook," Lewis said simply.

Allen rumpled his hair again, and his voice was fretful. "I don't get it. Do you expect to find her dead body?"

"I have an open mind," Lewis said tolerantly. "The suitcase is there with things which I believe are hers. I want to make sure that she is not in the house."

"You believe that the things are hers, but you can't be sure without Agatha's identification."

"Look." Lewis reminded himself of his position and tried to suppress his impatience. "I'm trying to save Miss Bunson. I can see that she's nervous and upset. I must search the house, and I don't want to have to get a warrant. I'd like to do it at once, and when I'm satisfied, I'll get out and stay out."

Allen looked at his watch. "All right. I'll see to it now. You want her permission for some time in the future, and then you want me to put her to sleep so that you can do it tonight."

"Right."

"I'll admit that I still can't see why Agatha has to be out of the way, but I'll do it for you."

Lewis relaxed on an easy breath of relief. Now he'd be able to get to the bottom of this thing. There was no doubt in his mind that Agatha knew all about it. He had seen people like her before. He put a match to his cigarette and moved restlessly around the room.

Mirrie came in and was delighted to see him. She had left Will in the hall and had told him sternly that he could not come in.

"Well!" She ran a hand over her curls. "You still here?"

Lewis smiled. "What did you think?"

Mirrie's hand in her curls became a little agitated. Driving in the wind, like that—if *only* her hair would take a decent permanent, but it was so *fine*.

Lewis talked easily, and they were getting along very well when Allen came back into the room. He gave Mirrie an absent nod and motioned Lewis into his office. He shut the door and said, "Well, you have her permission to search the place. She seemed almost pleased about it, which surprised me. Wanted to know when, and I told her some time soon, but she has work to do tonight which will keep her around until about eleven o'clock. Dr. Herser will give her the pill, because Agatha is her patient."

"Good." Lewis nodded. "I'll be back at eleven."

"What about Mr. Appely's room?"

Lewis did not know that Mr. Appely was a boarder, and Allen explained, "He'll be in his room from now until tomorrow morning, I should think. He bought a television set recently, and for the time being he stays with it."

"That's all right. I'll leave his room until tomorrow, and Miss Bunson's as well. Thanks a lot."

There was already one patient in the waiting room, and Mirrie was at her desk. Lewis did not stop, but they exchanged warm smiles as he passed through. In the hall he hesitated for a moment and then went back to the kitchen and peered in. Christine, Agatha, Will, and Fred were seated at the table drinking coffee, and they seemed to be engaged in an earnest conversation about plants and the best way to grow them. Lewis listened briefly and then got bored and took himself off.

Christine chatted along with the rest of them, but her attention was almost wholly on Agatha. When she'd followed her to the kitchen after the attempt, by way of a brief good night, to clear the dining room, Agatha had been tense to the point of rigidity. Christine had stayed with her and had tried to help with the dishes, until she discovered that it was only making things worse. Christine was *paying* for her meal, Agatha had said agitatedly. It was not *right* for her to be drying dishes.

In the end Christine retired to a chair and smoked a cigarette. Fred had appeared first, and Agatha was immediately reminded that she had forgotten him again. She had to pull things out of the ice chest and warm them up, and then Christine had suggested that they sit down and have some coffee. "You didn't have any at dinner, Miss Bunson. You left the entire cup."

Agatha looked at her and murmured limply, "Yes, I guess that's right. I'd like some coffee."

Allen had come in after that, and he'd talked quietly to Agatha and then had steered Christine into the hall and had talked to her. When Christine returned to the kitchen, she'd realized that Agatha was relaxed, more relaxed than she had ever seen her.

Will had come in, and Agatha offered him coffee. He was surprised, but he sat down at once, and immediately Fred began to complain that he couldn't find as good a place as that closet for his plants.

Will was astounded. "Wotcha mean? A closet ain't no place to grow plants. They gotta have sun and rain."

Fred explained patiently, and Will interrupted him to tell how he used to get things rooted when he lived at home. Agatha opined that Will's way was very careless, and Christine observed that she would like to have a plant of some sort for her bay window.

Will left and returned to his boardinghouse, where he passed the time in phoning around trying to raise Em. Agatha tidied the kitchen and got out the ironing board, and to Christine's suggestion that she retire early she nodded brightly and agreed.

Christine sat patiently through a mound of ironing and then

ordered warm milk and a pill for her patient.

"Do I need the pill?" Agatha asked doubtfully.

"I'd advise it. You seem relaxed, and if you take it, I think you'll get the best night's sleep you've had for some time."

Agatha nodded and wondered whether her present peace was merely the resignation of the doomed. That man would search the place tomorrow, and the dreadful, empty chair in the closet would be found. It was better to have it cleared up, though. Whatever might be hidden in the house would be found, and then she would show them the note. Someone had signed Em's name, and surely the man, Lewis, all of them, would realize that Miss Bunson could never have killed her cook. She would not say anything. It wouldn't be necessary. Only, she must unlock the closet so that they could get in there.

She waited until Christine went off to get the pill, and then she slipped along the hall, took the key from her pocket, and unlocked the closet door. Her face puckered a little as the door slid open a crack. Really, Fred's plants had left a most unpleasant odor, horrid. He must never put them there again.

She returned to the kitchen and warmed some milk. She'd sleep well tonight, and tomorrow it would all be taken out of her hands. She would be through with it.

Christine returned with the pill, and when she had seen Agatha swallow it and drink the milk, she escorted her upstairs.

"Go to bed now. Let your bones droop and breathe deeply, and you'll be off in no time. I know you didn't get much sleep last night."

"Good night, Dr. Christine," Agatha said tranquilly. "Thank you very much. You've been most helpful."

Christine lingered in the hall and listened to the sounds of Agatha getting to bed. When she had satisfied herself that the light was out and Agatha quiet, she went down to the front hall and was surprised to find that it was ten past eleven.

Allen appeared from his office and asked, "Well?"

"It's all right. All your patients gone?"

Allen nodded.

"Mirrie?"

"She left about an hour ago."

"Where's the fellow, Lewis?"

Allen shrugged. "Be just like him not to turn up, now that we have everything ready. What did you give Agatha?"

"Never mind what I gave her. If I told you, you'd only say it was all wrong. Don't worry about her. She'll sleep. But what did you say to her tonight? After you left her she was as peaceful as a bowl of jelly."

"I merely got her permission for Lewis to search the house. I'd expected her to show some fight, but she agreed quite readily."

Christine frowned. "I don't get that at all. Why should everything be all right simply because Lewis is going to search the house?"

Allen rested his shoulders against the wall behind him and gave her a faint, superior smile. "I should think that would be obvious. She wants something found but can't produce it herself."

"Smart, ain'tcha?"

Allen stared at the ceiling. "I wonder if it could be Em."

Christine gave a little shudder and muttered, "Don't be silly. Em's left, suitcase and all."

Lewis had kept his secret, Allen reflected, and it was not for him to betray it. He moved away from the wall and said, "Why don't you invite me into your rooms so that we can wait for Lewis in comfort?"

"Of course." She turned toward her door. "Only, I don't know what you mean by comfort. You won't be able to just sit. You'll find something wrong with the arrangements, and you'll have to fix it."

"Did Julia find anything wrong with my suggestions?" he demanded.

"She didn't notice anything. She was too busy talking."

"She didn't notice anything because nothing was wrong. Anyway, I'm tired tonight. I'm not going to do anything but sit and stare into space."

"Why on earth don't you go to bed?"

He shook his head. "I'm going to hang onto Lewis's coattails. I want to see what's up."

"Can't I hang onto yours?"

"No. Stay put, and I'll let you know if anything happens."

"Feeble female stuff. What *do* you expect to find?"

Allen slumped down into his chair and closed his eyes, and she regarded him coldly until the sound of the front door opening diverted her attention. She heard someone go upstairs, and she went over and shook Allen roughly.

"Lewis just came in, and he's gone on up."

Allen stumbled to his feet and made for the door. "What's the matter with him? He was supposed to wait for me."

They went out into the hall and met Lewis coming in the front door. He was a little breathless, and he asked, "Who was the young lady that just came in here?"

Chapter 19

CHRISTINE and Allen looked at each other and then at Lewis.

Allen said, "We didn't see any young lady. We heard someone come in and go upstairs, and we thought it was you."

"No, no. It was a young woman. Can't you tell me who it might be?"

"Are you sure it wasn't Mr. Appely?" Allen asked.

Christine giggled until they stared her back into silence.

"It was not Mr. Appely," Lewis said impatiently, "nor was it Miss Agatha. Who else has a room upstairs?"

"Nobody." Allen frowned thoughtfully. "Perhaps Julia dropped in to see a T.V. show on Mr. Appely's screen."

"At this hour?" Christine murmured.

"It wasn't the redhead," Lewis declared, "and it wasn't that blond one, Mirrie."

"Perhaps we're embarrassing the doctor," Christine suggested. "Might have been one of his girlfriends."

"I have no girlfriend who would walk in at this hour and go up to my room," Allen said furiously.

But Lewis was impressed. He nodded sagely and tried to be very tactful. "Perhaps you'd better investigate, Dr. Gremson. You never know about girls. They do strange things at times. You might just take a look, and I'll wait outside. Wouldn't want to walk in on the young person in full force."

Allen was fuming, but he allowed himself to be urged up to his room and pushed inside. He came out again almost immediately with a stony face.

"There is no one there, as I knew there wouldn't be."

Lewis knew that he hadn't looked properly, and he said mildly, "May I?" and slid in through the door. He looked in the closets and under the bed while Allen watched him from the hall.

"What about the bureau drawers?"

Lewis smiled with all the friendly charm that he could muster. "Suppose we go to the top floor and start the search."

Allen wanted to tell him to go and do it himself, but he was too anxious to see what was going on, so he swallowed his anger and led the way upstairs. He noticed that the steps were very clean, although they were rarely used. Agatha and Em had always gone to the back stairs. These were carpeted with the same strong, dark material that went all the way down to the main floor, and they were architecturally graceful. Allen wondered why Agatha didn't rent some of the attic rooms. It would mean extra cleaning, of course, and she simply could not force herself to accept help with it. No one else would do things in precisely the right way.

Christine had been waiting in a dim corner of the second-floor hall. She had listened at Agatha's door and heard nothing, and when the two men went up to the attic she followed quietly. She knew that if they noticed her they'd send her back.

Lewis was efficient and methodical. "I was up here most of the afternoon, and I looked around a bit, but I'll do it thoroughly now."

Allen slumped against the wall and watched him. He realized after a while that it was going to be an all-night job, and a very tiresome one. Lewis was opening drawers, trunks, and suitcases, and his search was slow and careful. Some of the rooms were empty, but there was Em's room, and one or two others which were partly furnished, and there was the trunk room, which was a long job all by itself.

Allen yawned, stretched, groaned, and at last gave up. "I'll have to leave you to it. I need some sleep. I've work to do in the morning."

Lewis glanced at him. "Yes, of course. Will you show me the rooms on the second floor first, the ones that I may go into?"

They went down, and Allen pointed out Agatha's room and Mr. Appely's. Lewis thanked him and said, "I'll not disturb you tonight either, nor the lady doctor."

Allen retired with his eyes already drooping, and Christine emerged from the shadows. "You can go through my rooms now if you want to."

Lewis jumped, since he had not been aware of her, but he was able to bow with aplomb. "Thanks very much. I'll just look through briefly, and then you can go to bed. You moved in very recently, didn't you?"

Christine nodded, and when they reached her rooms she suggested that he sit down for a moment.

"Well—" He sighed. "I'll take a break and have a cigarette with you."

She gave him a cup of coffee, too, and observed that it would help to keep him awake. "What are you searching for?" she asked, pouring a cup for herself.

"Nothing in particular. Anything that will help me to locate the missing cook."

He did not stay long, and he didn't bother to look through her rooms. He felt that it wasn't necessary. He went back to the third floor with his mind on the two things for which he was searching: Em, and Em's securities. He was relieved to be rid of Allen since he much preferred to work alone.

He went into Em's room. He hadn't liked to pull the bed apart under Allen's eyes, but now he stripped it and examined the mattress. There was only an open spring, so that the job did not take too long, but Em's securities were not there. He sighed and remade the bed carefully.

When he did find them at last, he was conscious of a sense of shame. Em had hidden her fortune in two manila envelopes, with advertisements on the outside, and they lay carelessly on top of a pile of magazines. Lewis had noticed them before but had assumed that they contained folders with further advertising. He reminded himself to overlook nothing, no matter how seemingly unimportant, in the future, and spread the contents out on the bed.

He whistled softly and shook his head. These were not negotiable, so why was Em worried about them? And the ghost had moved them and saved them from the robber? He shook his head again. She may have cashed some last year to get a profit in shining money, but she had plenty left. Too much. She could not possibly have amassed this from her salary. There was no cash, and he noticed Mr. Appely's neat signature on the one item.

He sat down in a chair and stared at the papers that fanned out across the bed. Had the stuff been planted up here, with the cash missing? Somebody wanted cash. Em had been looking for her securities, but she must have found them since she had said that the ghost had moved them for her and saved them from a thief. The ghost was Agatha walking in her sleep, of course, but Em knew only that they had been moved and that she had found them. Had she brought them up to her room and discovered that the cash was missing? Or had the cash been taken after Em was missing?

Lewis left his chair abruptly and scooped the papers back into their envelopes. He replaced them on the magazines and stood looking down at the floor for a thoughtful moment. He must find Em herself. The suitcase had been taken from its place in the trunk room, with some of her clothes in it, and put to one side so that everyone would think she had left. It seemed impossible that she could still be in the house and absurd that she would leave without the packed suitcase.

He went on with his search and eventually worked down to the second floor. There were two unoccupied rooms here, one a bedroom with maple furniture, gay chintz at the windows, and a matching bedspread. The drawers and closets were empty, and Lewis wondered why Agatha did not rent it at a good price. It was such a cheerful, pretty atmosphere.

The other room seemed to be a sort of den and was much smaller. There was a desk, an old-fashioned leather sofa, and glass-fronted bookcases. Rows of austere-looking books were lined up behind the glass, but there was nothing in the drawers of the desk or in the closet.

Lewis finished with the second floor and made his way downstairs. He hesitated in the lower hall, and then shrugged. No use going into the doctor's office. He'd look around in the kitchen and then go on down to the cellar.

Christine emerged from her door wearing a sweeping robe of an odd dull-green color, with matching slippers. She pushed soft hair back from her forehead and smiled at him. "I heard you come down, and I wondered whether you'd found anything."

Lewis thought she looked charming and lied to her with all the polish at his command. "No, no. Nothing yet."

"Where are you going now?"

"I thought I'd take a look around the kitchen."

Christine followed him. She knew that he wanted to be alone, but she stood in the middle of the kitchen while he went into the little sitting room. She was seated in a chair by the time he got to the various kitchen closets, and when he had finished those he came over, brushing at his suit, and offered her a cigarette. "Nothing on this floor, I guess. I'll do the cellar next."

"How about some coffee before you start?"

Lewis nodded and murmured, "Love it."

Christine knew the kitchen well enough by now to find what she wanted, and after she had put the coffee on the stove she returned to her chair.

"Did you know anyone in the household before you moved here?" Lewis asked.

Christine said, "No," and then remembered Allen. "I mean, I knew Dr. Gremson some years ago, that's all."

"I see." But he didn't, really. He had no idea of what was actually going on around here.

Christine cupped her chin in her palm. "Did you ever look in that closet under the stairs in the front hall?"

Lewis was annoyed with himself, but he answered honestly enough, "No, I didn't know there was one. I hadn't noticed it."

"You can't get into it, anyway. It's locked."

"There's a drawer full of keys here. One of them might fit." He went over to the drawer and began to rummage with a rather agitated hand. "This is enough to start with. Where's the closet?"

Christine led him along the hall and indicated the door. He stooped to examine the lock, and then fingered through the keys until he found one that he thought might do. He was about to insert it when he frowned suddenly and turned the knob. The door was open.

He pulled, and a bar of light from the hall moved across the inert body of a young girl.

Chapter 20

A FOUL ODOR seeped from the open door of the closet, and Lewis took a step backward. Christine urged him out of her way with a hand on his arm, and dropped to her knees beside the girl. "Can you get some more light here?"

"No, leave her. I'll shut the door and call the station. The smell—"

"She's warm," Christine said sharply. "I think she's alive. Help me to get her out."

Lewis lifted the limp body and kicked the door shut with his foot. Christine said, "Wait a minute. I want to see—" But he walked back to the kitchen and into the little sitting room and put the girl on a couch.

"No light back there," he said briefly, and made no mention of the fact that he had been anxious to get this stranger away from the hall before anyone saw her.

Christine leaned over the couch, and Lewis muttered, "She's been hit on the back of the head. There's blood on my suit."

"Yes." Christine straightened up. "You wait here. I'll have to get some things. It's no accident. Someone struck her."

Lewis nodded. He'd seen the wound and had come to the same conclusion himself. He moved restlessly about the small room while he waited for Christine to return, his hands jammed in his pockets and his mind on the closet. She was there, all right—Em. That odor. Must be a good closet, well sealed. You couldn't smell anything until you opened the door.

Christine came back, and he stopped pacing and said tentatively, "Perhaps I had better get Miss Agatha to help you."

"No, no. Let her sleep. She needs it badly. This girl isn't too bad. Just give me a hand here while I patch her up, and then we'll get her to bed somewhere."

Lewis moved to her side and protested at the same time, "But I'll have to telephone—"

"I know—but this won't take a minute. Look—hold her this way."

Lewis gave in and helped in silence. When they had finished, he said, "Stay here with her. I'll be back soon," and hurried along to the closet. He opened the door and snapped on his flashlight, and the beam picked up the empty rocking chair at the back. He lowered it and saw the outlines of Em's huddled body. Well, that was that. She'd been left in the rocking chair, and the body had fallen sideways to the floor.

He backed out and closed the door. He prowled the hall for some time before he was convinced that there was no phone there, and at last he went back to the kitchen. The coffee was bubbling over on the stove, so he turned it low.

"I want to get her to bed," Christine said from the sitting room. "I wonder who she is. She doesn't seem to have a purse. Perhaps it's in the closet where she was lying."

"I'll have a look," Lewis replied, and was annoyed with himself once more. He should have searched for a purse, but the sight of Em had knocked everything else out of his mind. "Er—where is the phone here?"

Christine shook her head. "I really don't know, but you can use mine. The door's open."

Lewis went first to the closet, but although he looked carefully with the aid of his flashlight, he could not find a purse. He searched the floor of the hall just outside, found nothing, and at last went to the telephone in Christine's office.

When he returned to the kitchen, Christine was still in the sitting room by her patient, and she was sipping coffee. "I put a cup on the table there for you," she told him. "Just pour it out."

He nodded and filled the cup from the pot on the stove. There was nothing more for him to do now until they came, and then the thing would be out of his hands. He had found Em, but his superior would take over at this point.

"I found a blanket for her," Christine said, nodding at the still unconscious girl. "Matter of fact, I think it would be better if she could stay where she is for a while. She's so small that she fits quite comfortably on this couch."

THE LITTLES   101

"Is there anything in her pockets?" Lewis asked. "I couldn't find any purse."

"There aren't any pockets in her dress, but that little jacket she was wearing might have some. Over there on the chair."

Lewis found two pockets in the short blue jacket, but one was empty, and the other contained only a soiled handkerchief. He flung the jacket over the back of a chair and said abstractedly, "I'll have to wake Miss Agatha and see whether she can identify the girl."

"What's the hurry?" Christine asked. "I think the girl will be all right now, and the few hours until morning won't make much difference."

Lewis cleared his throat. "I'll have to get her up, anyway. They'll be here any minute now."

"They?"

"I found Em in the closet."

Christine put down her coffee cup with a little clatter and got to her feet, staring at him. "What!"

Lewis nodded. "Been dead for some time. I didn't look too closely, but I think she was hit on the head too."

"Oh God, how awful!" Christine muttered. "You mean she's been in there all along?"

"I don't know how long she's been there." He glanced at the clock over the sink and added, "I'd like you to go up and wake Miss Agatha and bring her down here."

Christine shook her head. "I gave her a pill, on your instructions, if you'll remember. You'll have to leave her alone for a while. I'm her doctor, and I won't have her disturbed just yet."

Lewis shrugged. "The boss will want to know what's the matter with her."

"I don't mind telling the boss what's the matter with her. She's been walking in her sleep, and the reason she walks in her sleep dates all the way back to her father. He seems to have taken pleasure in twisting her mind up like a pretzel. I'm endeavoring to untwist her, but it isn't exactly a simple job to straighten out a pretzel."

Lewis gave her a fleeting smile and then wiped it off. "I'd better go to the front door so that I can let them in. They should be here by now. Could you get in touch with Kroning?"

"I don't know where he lives," Christine said.

"In a rooming house. I thought you might know the address."

Christine didn't, and he presently went out to the front hall. The door was unlocked, and the catch was so stiff that he assumed it was not often used. It had to be left open for the patients, of course, and it was probable that no one bothered to lock it at night.

It was daylight when Agatha awoke, and she made little stretching movements with a sense of relaxation and pleasure. She could not remember when she had had such a good sleep, and she felt rested and well. She lay for a while, blinking contentedly at the window, and then suddenly the familiar tension gripped her stomach. That man was going to search the house. Would he find Em? Perhaps not. She wasn't in the chair. Somebody must have taken her away. If they never found her it wouldn't matter. It would be good. Only, she must be somewhere. Had she simply walked out of the closet and away? Oh no, she musn't let these morbid thoughts slip into her head and frighten her. Someone had killed Em. She was dead, and someone had removed her body from the closet.

Agatha's eyes moved to the clock, and she flung out of bed in a panic. It was late. She had barely time to dress and prepare the breakfast. But Fred would be there, and he'd put the coffee on for her.

Her first glimpse of the kitchen filled her with anger and dismay. It was dirty! The floor was filthy!

Fred Slupp was there, and he had put the coffee on. His face was strange with an unaccustomed look of excitement, and he forgot to say good morning. "I thought you'd be sleeping the day away, miss, and all that's been going on here. Enough to put the fear of God into the devil himself."

"What?" Agatha whispered. "What is it?"

"It's Em they've found—dead, and may she rest well—and right in the very closet where I've been keeping me plants."

Agatha's hands writhed together, and she stared at Fred in silence. How could they have found Em there? How *could* they? The rocking chair had been empty. She had seen it with her own eyes.

"Now, don't take on, miss," Fred said, looking at her white face. "It's nothing you can help, and I'm thinking they'll not bother you too much. As for meself, they had me out of me bed before the day broke, and did I know the girl, and who hit her on the head, as though it wasn't their own job to find out, the lazy devils. I told them. I said, 'When she comes to herself, she'll speak for herself.' But the empty-headed fools will listen to no voices but their own."

"What are you talking about?" Agatha gasped. "Who was hit? Was it the lady doctor?"

"No, no, not her, but another one, and who she is they don't know and can't get a soul to tell them either."

Agatha advanced on him and clutched at his shoulder with a thin, shaking hand. "But I don't know what you're talking about. I don't understand you. Tell me—can't you tell me?"

Fred eased away from her. "I don't know who she is, and so I told them, but it may be that you will know. It's in your sitting room she is."

Agatha whirled and opened the sitting-room door with the flat of her hand. Christine was asleep in a chair, and the girl still lay on the couch, but she was moving a little, and as Agatha looked, her eyelids fluttered.

Agatha gave an exclamation, and Christine woke up. She got out of her chair quickly and said, "Sit down. Do you know the girl?"

Agatha remained on her feet. "Who is she? What happened to her?"

"Wallop on the head," Christine explained briefly. "She'll be all right."

Agatha's face was gray, and the motion of her hands never ceased. She asked huskily, "Where's Em?"

"They've taken her away. I'm sorry—"

"The funeral," Agatha muttered. "She must have a good funeral. I shall see to it."

Unexpectedly the girl on the couch said, "Godalmighty!"

Christine turned to her at once. "How do you feel?"

The girl gave her a blank stare and then asked, "Where's Ma?"

"She's coming."

"Yeah? Gee-zuz! Wotta head I got!"

"You lie still and keep it flat," Christine said firmly. She glanced at Agatha and then went over and disentangled her hands. "Relax, Miss Agatha. You really must. Breathe slowly and deeply, and let yourself sag."

Agatha backed away. "I can't—the breakfast. It's late now."

"Never mind the breakfast. Everything is upside down this morning, anyway. No one will expect the usual service."

"But—but, this girl—what shall I do?"

"You need not concern yourself about the girl at all," Christine explained. "They'll take her to the hospital sometime this morning."

Agatha turned away and said vaguely, "I'll have some coffee—it's on. It must be ready by now."

She plunged into the kitchen and bumped into Fred, who was standing just outside the door. He said, "Sorry, miss," and took himself over to the sink with guilty haste.

Agatha scarcely noticed him. The girl—that girl in there—

she had been hit on the head, just like Em, only not so hard, and not in the same spot. What had been used this time? She'd have to go upstairs and see whether the gun was still there.

Will walked into the kitchen with his hair on end and his face unshaven. He said, "Gimme a cuppa corfee, for Godsakes. Where's this here girl I'm supposed to take a gander at."

Agatha gestured toward the sitting room, and he crossed the kitchen and went through the doorway. His voice rose almost immediately in an alarmed bellow.

"What the hell! It's Ginny."

Chapter 21

LEWIS appeared in the doorway of the sitting room, and there was about him an indefinable air of importance. He seemed cloaked in a new authority—, nd was. The boss was sick, and he'd been put in charge of this case, and he intended to show them—all of them.

He said to Will, "This your sister? Ginny?"

Will was shaking the girl's arm, and Christine said sharply, "Leave her alone. She's all right. She's sleeping."

"What happened to her?" Will demanded.

"Someone hit her on the head."

"Or she fell against something," Lewis said smoothly.

Christine opened her mouth to refute this and then closed it again. Lewis must be up to something, since he knew perfectly well that the girl could not have got that wound by falling in the closet.

Allen and Mr. Appely came into the kitchen. They had been up since five, had answered many of Lewis's questions, and they were tired and hungry. They looked at each other gloomily. It appeared that if they wanted breakfast they'd have to make it for themselves.

Mr. Appely brightened suddenly and moved over to the door of the sitting room. "Miss Christine," he said timidly, "perhaps *you* could make some breakfast."

Christine yawned and shook her head. "Can't leave my patient—all these people milling around. Cook me some bacon and eggs, will you? And coffee. And don't forget the orange juice. I want to stay here until they take her to the hospital."

Will swung around with fire in his eye. "Ginny ain't goin' to no hospital! Ma'll move in here and take care of her. Ma don't wear no fancy white cap, nor she don't make you feel worse by sloshing alcohol all over you and talkin' cheerful when you feel like hell. Us Kronings don't hold with hospitals."

Christine yawned again. "Don't be an idiot. She'll have the best of care, and she won't be in long, in any case."

"She won't be in at all." Will slapped his hat onto his head. "I'm goin' out to phone Ma now, and if Ginny ain't here when I get back I'll make it hot for somebody."

He flung into the kitchen and came face to face with Agatha. "I'm gonna phone Ma," he told her belligerently. "I won't have my sister in no hospital, see? I want to rent a room from you for Ma and Ginny until Ginny gets well."

"Your sister?" Agatha said vaguely. "But what do you mean? Oh—the girl. She's your sister?"

"When I get my hands on the guy who done all this," Will said through his teeth, "he'll wisht he'd been drowned when his old lady took the first look at him. You gimme a room, huh? I gotta phone Ma."

Agatha shook her head, and a worried frown creased her forehead. "I really don't know what to say. I mean, I don't exactly—"

Will said quickly. "That's swell! I'll carry Ginny into any room you say when I get back. I'm goin' down to the corner. I don't want to run up bills on nobody's phone around here."

He departed in a great hurry, although Agatha called after him faintly, "I don't know about a room. I really don't think— You could use my phone, in the upstairs hall—"

He had gone before she finished speaking, and she began to move around the kitchen, starting preparations for breakfast.

This girl, Will's sister, it seemed—why had she come here? Would Will injure his own sister? Of course if this Ginny were dead, Will would probably get all the money. Only, it seemed dreadful to think of him trying to kill his sister. And yet murders within families had happened often enough.

Allen could see that her mind was not on what she was doing, and he began to help her. He put cutlery and cups and saucers on the kitchen table, and presently he and Mr. Appely were relaxing over hot coffee and bacon and eggs.

Christine walked in and said doubtfully, "I suppose we can't send the girl to the hospital after what that fellow said."

Allen looked up. "No, you'll have to leave it to him. She's not too bad, anyway, is she?"

"Oh no. But there's too much traffic around here. I want to get her bedded down somewhere in peace and quiet."

"Where's Lewis?"

"He's in there waiting for her to talk. Listen, how about some food? I'm starving."

Allen nodded toward Agatha, who was at the stove. "Just get a plate and shovel some of the stuff on. She's in a trance."

Christine sent a quick glance at Agatha and then went over and spoke to her. There was no reply except an absentminded, interrogative murmur, and Christine turned away to get herself a plate. She filled it and sat down at the kitchen table. Agatha was in a trance, all right, but the tightness had gone out of her, and Christine could have sworn that she was relieved about something. Only, what? She'd followed Agatha down yesterday morning and had seen her with her hand on that door of the closet under the stairs. The door had been locked, but had Agatha known of the gruesome thing that lay beyond it? Oh, she must have known. It explained all that nervous tension, and now she'd loosened up because Em had been found.

Will banged in through the kitchen door and slowed up when he saw them eating. "Gee-zuz! I got a hole in my belly like all outdoors." He moved over to the stove and said to Agatha, "Ma'll be here in a couple hours. Show me what room I can take Ginny to, huh?"

Agatha gave him a brief glance. "I have no room."

"I know you got one," Will said earnestly. "Up on the second floor there. You and the doc and Mr. Appely is the only ones on that floor, so I know you got a spare room. Come on, Miss Agatha, don't be a lemon. You wouldn't want to get hauled off to one of them hospitals yourself, would you?"

"Certainly not." Agatha gave an impatient little sigh and then stared down at the two eggs that lay in the frying pan. A faint nausea stirred in her stomach, and she turned away abruptly, leaving the eggs where they were. She took a cup and saucer from the shelf, poured coffee, and sat down at a corner of the kitchen table.

Will looked after her and then back at the frying pan. He asked, "Anyone want these?" and when he received no answer, fetched a plate and scooped the eggs onto it. He sat down with the others, disposed of the eggs in exactly four mouthfuls, and then drained, without taking breath, a cup of coffee that Christine had poured for him. He sighed vastly, curtained a belch with a discreet hand, and lighted a cigar.

"How about that room, Miss Agatha? I told Ma it was all right, and you wouldn't want to make me out a liar."

"Oh, don't bother me!" Agatha said impatiently. "You can use my sister's room. She isn't likely to be back. But there's only one bed there, and you'll need two."

"Don't you worry none about beds," Will told her eagerly. "I seen some stored up on the third floor, and I'll bring one down."

Agatha pressed her closed eyes with the tips of her fingers. "Very well, as long as you attend to it yourself."

"I'll help you," Allen offered.

"Thanks, Doc." Will extinguished his cigar on the egg plate and stood up. "I'll carry Ginny up now, and then we'll get the bed down for Ma."

"Oh no!" Agatha's eyes flew open. "I must clean that room first, and make the bed. You'll have to leave her where she is until the room is ready. Get the other bed down. I'll show you which one, and then I'll start cleaning right away. After I've done the dishes, of course."

"Don't bother about the dishes," Christine said quickly. "I'll attend to them. You go on off and fix the room. The sooner we get Ginny moved, the better."

Agatha looked doubtful and was inclined to hang back, but Allen urged her out of the room with a hand on her shoulder.

Christine had started to carry dishes to the sink when Lewis appeared and asked diffidently if he might have some breakfast. She nodded, cracked two eggs into the pan, and was a little put out to discover that both yokes had broken. She decided that they'd look better scrambled and began to stir them around with a fork.

Lewis sat down at the table. "The girl's asleep again. I thought she was ready to talk, but she didn't say anything more."

"She'll talk before long," Christine said absently, and reflected that it was a good thing she did not, herself, have to eat the mess she was cooking up. She presently passed it across to Lewis, who ate it with every appearance of enjoyment. He drank coffee and then pulled out a cigarette.

"Somebody should be with that girl all the time. Could you take over while I do some phoning?"

"Of course, but I think she'll be all right now. I'll get these dishes done and look in on her occasionally."

"I don't believe you quite understand me," Lewis said, turning his cigarette in his fingers. "Someone attacked her, but she's still alive. Whoever it was may want to finish the job before she starts talking."

Christine widened her eyes at him and said quietly, "I hadn't thought of that."

"No, but it must be considered. I won't be long, and I rely on you to watch her closely."

Christine nodded, and he left, trying to keep his aspect modest even though he was now boss man on the case.

Christine glanced into the sitting room where the girl was sleeping quietly and then gathered the dishes together and started washing them. Fred Slupp came in, and she turned quickly, but he merely picked up a towel and began to dry for her. He found a plate with a piece of egg still adhering to it and handed it back. Christine washed it again and had just finished it when he returned a cup which had a bit of crystallized sugar in the bottom. She flipped water from her hands, dried them, and said grimly, "Suppose you wash."

Fred was surprised. "It's not a job I'm knowing much about, but I don't mind obliging you, miss, just this once."

Lewis came back and was followed shortly by Mirrie. Her face was pink with excitement, and she was a little breathless.

"I just got here and heard about it. Isn't it awful?"

"Who told you?" Lewis asked.

"Why, Mr. Appely, I met him down the street." She paused, and turned her head toward the door in an attitude of listening. "Oh gee, wouldn't you know it? Somebody just went into the waiting room. I'll have to go."

She hurried along the hall and met Agatha, Allen, and Will descending the stairs.

"But it don't make no difference," Will was saying in an exasperated voice. "Ginny ain't gonna care if the ceiling was dusted today or next year. I gotta get her up there. Doc says she needs to be quiet."

"I cannot allow anyone to move into that room until it is properly clean," Agatha declared. "The woodwork must be washed, for one thing. You'll simply have to give me a little time."

Mirrie stared, and Allen turned her around and pushed her into the waiting room. Will went straight on through to the kitchen, into the sitting room, and lifted his sister from the sofa. He carried her upstairs, followed by Agatha, Christine, and Lewis. As he lowered her to the bed he saw that her eyes were open, and she turned her head from side to side in a bewildered fashion.

"Where's Ma?"

"Ma's comin'," Will told her. "Listen, kid. Who done this to you?"

"It was that crazy old bat, Agatha," Ginny said, and closed her eyes.

Chapter 22

CHRISTINE, Lewis, and Will turned to look at Agatha, but this time she did not worry her hands. She balled them into fists and said in a clear voice, "The girl is telling a lie. I did not hit her."

"Ginny don't tell lies," Will said ominously.

Agatha spat back at him, "She's telling one now, because I never touched her."

"Perhaps you were walking in your sleep, Miss Bunson," Lewis suggested.

"Oh no." Agatha's eyes flashed around to Christine. "You know I didn't walk last night. You gave me a pill, and I slept soundly. I always know when I've been walking, and I did not leave my bed last night."

Christine nodded. "I think that's right. The girl must be mistaken."

Lewis and Will turned back to Ginny, but she seemed to be sleeping again, and Lewis sighed. "I suppose we'd better leave her. Will you stay with her, Dr. Herser, until her mother arrives?"

Christine agreed, and Lewis urged the others out of the room. He came back to whisper briefly, "See if you can find out whether she's certain that it was Miss Agatha," and Christine gave him an understanding nod.

Agatha was furious. She knew very well that she had not touched that vulgar girl, and yet people seemed determined to blame her for everything. It had always been that way, though, always! Her face pinched under a wave of self-pity.

She went to the kitchen and cleaned it thoroughly, and then she took a pail of water and ammonia to the front hall and began to wash the stair carpeting. She worked doggedly, her mind blank save for a dull preoccupation with the job, and had only two stairs left to do when Mrs. Kroning arrived.

Agatha thought she was one of Allen's patients and ignored her.

"May I speak to Miss Bunson?"

Agatha turned and stood up, her arm brushing hair back from her forehead. "I'm Miss Bunson. What is it?"

"I'm looking for my girl, Ginny."

Agatha's face soured a little as she observed this third member of the Kroning clan infesting her house. She said abruptly, "She's upstairs, but I've just washed the carpet here, and I don't want it used yet. I'll show you the back stairs."

Mrs. Kroning lowered her bag to the floor and seated herself in one of the hall chairs. "Thanks for nothing. I don't use nobody's back stairs. I'll wait until these dry."

Agatha shrugged and returned to her work. The woman was a coarse clod, like the other Kronings.

Mrs. Kroning settled into her chair, pulled her dress down over her fat knees, and then observed, "You ain't washing them steps right, you know it?"

The rag dropped from Agatha's hand, and she spun around, with her eyes blazing.

"See, I use a small brush *and* a rag," Mrs. Kroning explained comfortably. "You gotta scrub the carpet with the brush so you get the dirt up to the top. Then you wash it off with the rag."

"But I get the underneath dirt out with the vacuum cleaner first," Agatha protested agitatedly, "and then I go over it with the rag."

Mrs. Kroning compressed her lips and shook her head. "Well, it ain't my house or my business, but I happen to know that the cleaner don't get the deep dirt out. I always find plenty when I use the brush."

No one had ever criticized Agatha's cleaning before, but her annoyance was diluted by an uneasy doubt. She finished the last step in silence and then stood up and turned around.

"I vacuum often enough so that there is no imbedded dirt in my carpets."

She picked up the pail and headed swiftly for the kitchen, but Mrs. Kroning had a carrying voice, and it came clearly to her ears.

"*I* vacuum *every* day."

Just inside the kitchen door Agatha shut her teeth together and hissed to herself, "Liar!" How could the woman find time to vacuum every day? She vacuumed twice a week, herself, and on the other days she used a clean carpet sweeper. She was busy all the time, anyway. How could she do any more? Chances were those Kronings hadn't more than two rugs in the entire house, so of course she could go over them every day. She lived out in the country, too, where there was plenty of mud to be tracked in, so it was no wonder that she found dirt in her cheap rugs.

Agatha returned to the front hall, with the express purpose of accusing Mrs. Kroning of having only two rugs, and was horrified to discover that she was no longer there. She had gone up, dirtying the carpet before it was dry! After she had been told to wait!

Agatha flew to the back stairs, her breath whistling fiercely through her throat. She climbed swiftly and burst into the room in which Ginny lay, and was in time to hear Mrs. Kroning say firmly to Christine, "I got to clean this room thoroughly if Ginny is gonna stay here."

Agatha's chest swelled, but Christine spoke before she could assort a torrent of angry words.

"The room was cleaned, most thoroughly, before your daughter was brought in here. As long as I am taking care of her I must insist that there be no more cleaning before tomorrow morning. By that time I expect her to be feeling pretty well again."

Mrs. Kroning sniffed and glanced at the girl on the bed. "Will insisted on me comin' here," she complained, "although I can't for the life of me see why. He said Ginny bumped her head against a door. So she's always crackin' her arm or her leg or her head at home, and no harm done. I got work to do out at the house, and I hadda drop everything to traipse over here and give her an aspirin. Why don't she look where she's goin', anyways?"

"It's probable that he didn't want to alarm you too much on the phone," Christine said, "but it really is worse than that. Someone struck your daughter, and she has a slight concussion. She's lucky that it was not more serious. Your son did not want her to go to the hospital—"

"Horspital!" Mrs. Kroning settled her girdle with a couple of indignant jerks. "I should say not!" She moved over toward the bed, and the girl opened her eyes.

"What you yappin' about, Ma?"

Mrs. Kroning was inclined to be severe. "What in time did you come to this house for, Ginny? What are you up to now? I know you got some bee buzzing around in your bonnet, and I want to know all about it."

"Aw, Ma." Ginny's lids dropped over her eyes. "Leave me be, will you? I feel like hell."

Mrs. Kroning had every intention of sifting the matter to the bottom at once, but Christine laid a hand on her arm and drew her over to the other side of the room. Agatha was still in the doorway, and Christine urged her out and closed the door. She returned her attention to Mrs. Kroning and talked to her in a clipped, professional voice that she reserved for special occasions. She talked to the point, wasting no words, and in the end Mrs. Kroning was almost, if not quite, cowed. She promised to guard and attend her daughter to the best of her ability, and added with a little flash of spirit that she'd always done the best by her children, and that without the say-so of a snippy young piece who might be a doctor but who certainly wasn't dry behind the ears yet—see!

Christine went downstairs and reported to Lewis, who was upsetting the neatness and order of Agatha's little sitting room by an apparently aimless rummage.

"I'd like to go to bed now," Christine concluded.

"Certainly. Of course."

She went off quickly, half afraid that he would call her back. Her eyes were drooping, and she was desperate for sleep. She pushed through the door of her waiting room and felt a sagging of her whole body when she beheld Julia sitting in a chair, smoking a cigarette.

"My dear, I thought you'd never come! I couldn't go pushing in with everyone around, so I came here to wait for you and get the dirt."

"How did you know there was any dirt to get?"

Julia tapped ash from her cigarette with a long red fingernail. "Darling, the mailman. He brought the letters into the front hall as usual and heard things going on. So when he got to me, of course he asked me."

Christine sat down and rubbed her temples with her fingertips. "What did he hear?"

"Oh, things. And then Mirrie came into the hall and mentioned murder, so of course he was all excited. I promised to find out all about it and let him know tomorrow."

Christine picked up a cigarette, decided that she didn't want it, and then found herself smoking it. "It's Em. They found her body in a closet, skull smashed in. There was a young girl there too, also conked on the head, but not so hard. She's alive and will soon be battling with her mother. She turned out to be Will Kroning's sister."

Julia gave a little gasp and whispered, "My God! Who did it?"

Christine shrugged.

"But that's awful!" Julia stared down at the tip of her cigarette. "I suppose poor old Agatha has cracked wide open at last. Em always did frazzle her until she was ready to scream."

Christine glanced up. "Em?"

"Oh yes. You know how Agatha takes to cleaning the way some people take to the bottle, and Em was what you might call a comfortable slattern."

Christine nodded. "Agatha seems to have been under the impression that she couldn't get rid of her."

"I know. But look, what was Will's sister doing here?"

"I've no idea."

There was a knock on the door, and Will walked in without waiting to be bidden. When he saw Julia he stopped and said, "Oh."

Julia looked up at him. "I'm terribly sorry about your aunt."

"Yeah, too bad." Will turned to Christine. "I'm telling you, that dame is gonna pay for knockin' Ginny cold and dumpin' her in the closet. You heard what Ginny said. You was there, and I want you to sign a paper sayin' you heard it."

"What?" Julia cried eagerly. "What did Ginny say? Does she know who hit her?"

"Ginny says it was Agatha, and I'm tellin' you, the crazy old bat ought to be put away, and I'm gonna see she is put away. Her old man always said she was nuts. Em told me so, and he oughta known if anybody did."

"I believe her father was being deliberately cruel," Christine said quietly. "He did not care for her and treated her badly. But she's not insane, and I don't think for an instant that she hit your sister."

Will's face reddened, and his voice rose. "What in hell are you talkin' about? You heard Ginny say she did."

"Yes, but I believe she was mistaken. After all, she doesn't know Agatha very well."

"She knows her good enough to pick her out in a crowd," Will declared angrily. "She come here to visit Em sometimes, and she seen her then."

"Will," Julia said pacifically, "why don't you let the police unravel this thing? You're all excited and upset, and it isn't doing you any good. The police will solve it, and the right person will be punished. Now, you come along with me to my office and sit down quietly and have a drink."

Will expelled a long breath, knuckled his forehead, and muttered, "I could use a drink."

"Good." Julia stood up. "Come along."

They went off, and Christine sighed vastly. "Thank God! Now I can get some sleep."

The door opened again, and Allen slid in.

"Want to know something? This Ginny is Em's daughter."

Chapter 23

CHRISTINE'S ANNOYANCE at being prevented from plunging straight into bed gave way to surprise and curiosity. "How did you learn that?" she demanded.

"I'd gone up to my room for something, and I heard Mrs. Kroning and the girl talking. I started to go in because I thought the girl might be needing some attention, but I stopped behind the half-opened door. I heard Ginny say to Mrs. Kroning that she'd come here to try and find Em. She said, 'After all, she *is* my mother.' Mrs. Kroning shushed her and said something about she wasn't to let anyone know that. The girl shut up, and I waited for a while and then went in. She was sleeping again, and the old dame was sitting by the bed, knitting."

"Was Lewis there?" Christine asked.

"No. The poor guy went off at the wrong time, I guess. I don't know whether we ought to tell him or not. Probably it's just a private scandal that has nothing to do with Em's death. I thought you ought to know, though, since the girl is your patient. Perhaps you can find out more about it, and then you can make up your mind about whether you should tell Lewis."

"I'll look in on her later when she's more awake," Christine agreed. "Thanks for the information. I'll see if I can dig up anything else."

Allen glanced around the room. "No patients yet?"

"I don't suppose you have morning office hours yourself," she said coldly.

"Once a week, and this is it. They're practically crawling up the walls over there. I can't handle them all. They're mostly women, and I wondered whether you'd mind if I sent some of them over here. Just a loan, you know, but you could use the business, and I'd get time to snatch some lunch eventually."

"Sure." Christine gave a yawn that ended in a groan. "Just the simple cases, naturally. Ingrown toenails and dandruff. I mean, I'm only a woman doctor and I wouldn't want to kill any of your wealthy chronics."

"Shut up," Allen said amiably. "I'm going back there now, and I'll weed out an assortment and send them over with their cards clutched in their grubby little fists."

He departed, and Christine made a face at the door. It would be wonderful to have some patients, but she hated having to take Allen's overflow. Damned superior male! She'd rather work up her own practice without any help from him.

She hastily tidied herself and her rooms, and then sat down in her office and tried to keep her eyes from closing. So Ginny was Em's daughter. Perhaps she should go up and see the girl now. Chances were that Allen had been joking about sending some patients over.

She heard the sound of a cough from the waiting room and went out to find three elderly ladies sitting there. They wore the usual blank expressions of waiting patients, but when she appeared one of them stood up immediately.

"Dr. Herser? Dr. Gremson sent me over. He wants you to examine me, you know. Such a wonderful man, Dr. Gremson, so tactful and considerate. Who else would think of employing a lady doctor to examine ladies? It has *always* upset me to have a man pawing over my body. So embarrassing."

Christine led the way to her office and reminded herself silently that a doctor must hold onto her temper at all costs.

Agatha had seen the three women leave Allen's office and walk across the hall, but she had given them only a passing, puzzled thought. She was washing the woodwork in the hall by this time, and she was burning with anger. The earlier peace of mind that had been so relaxing was gone entirely. That common, horrid Kroning girl—the impudence of her! Making wild accusations that were entirely untrue. And the stupid, fat mother, pretending that she knew so much about house cleaning! Agatha knew herself to be an expert in all matters of cleaning, and she intended to talk to that woman. She'd talk to the girl too. But the man, Lewis, had been hanging around in the bedroom, and she couldn't talk in front of him. He was in the kitchen now, though, with Fred. She couldn't leave with the woodwork still unfinished. She must hurry and try to get to the girl's bedroom before Lewis went up there again.

Lewis was still in the kitchen when she finished at last, but she had to empty the pail and hang the rag away, and she was afraid he would stop her and begin asking questions. But he merely gave her an abstracted nod and asked Fred if he knew the occupation of the man who owned the house across the street.

Agatha went quietly up the stairs and approached the Kroning girl's bedroom. The door was slightly ajar and there was no sound from inside, and after a moment's hesitation she gave a gentle knock and walked in.

Mrs. Kroning was knitting furiously, and she looked up at Agatha without breaking the rhythm of her needles. In her anger Agatha had neglected to assort her words into a coherent indictment, and she was silent while her mind darted from one agitated idea to another. Mrs. Kroning looked her straight in the eye and said, "Well?"

Agatha swallowed and succumbed to weakness. "Er—how is your daughter?"

Mrs. Kroning had been brought abreast of the facts, and she spoke coldly. "I guess you'll be sorry to hear that she's doin' fine, and you won't get another chance at her, neither. Don't you come a step nearer or I'll holler."

"I did not hit her. I never touched her," Agatha cried shrilly. "Dr. Herser knows that I had a sedative and that it kept me sleeping all night. And I would never have done such a dreadful thing, anyway!"

Mrs. Kroning said, "Hmm," over the rapid clicking of her needles.

Lewis had followed Agatha up and was standing just outside the door. He was feeling rather clever because he'd thought she might try to get to the girl again. He breathed lightly and strained his ears.

Agatha had thought up something to say and was delivering it with an air of triumph. "You are knitting much too fast. There are bound to be holes in your work if you keep up that speed."

Mrs. Kroning's busy hands became still, and her small hazel eyes seemed to glaze over with a layer of ice. She said in a low, deadly voice, "Will you be just good enough to walk yourself over here and take a look at my work? For every hole you find, I'll give you five dollars."

Agatha made a negative little gesture with her hand. "No, no—I—I'll take your word for it."

"Maybe you're the kind who has to go slow and careful and count out loud," Mrs. Kroning went on, "but that don't mean we're all dumb."

"I don't knit at all," Agatha said stiffly. "*I* have not the time."

"*I* make time."

Agatha had a wild feeling that she was being badly—and unfairly—worsted. "I have to make time even to keep the house up," she cried hotly. "You couldn't be expected to understand. I'm quite sure your house in the country is very much smaller than this place."

Mrs. Kroning's brow clouded a little as she thought of her neat six-room cottage, but a moment's thought brought a fitting reply to her lips.

"*You* do no baking or cooking."

"I do, now." Agatha protested. "Besides, when Em was here I spent more time cleaning up after her than it would have taken me to bake and cook."

Mrs. Kroning lowered her knitting into her lap, and her face underwent a change. Her voice dropped, and she said in a tone of confidence, "I never been one to speak ill of the dead, but I got to admit I don't know how you ever put up with a sloppy piece like Em." She shook her head from side to side. "You must have had a time of it, all right."

"Well!" Agatha drew a long breath. "I was ready to fly out of my skin. But just the same"—she looked Mrs. Kroning in the eye—"I had nothing to do with her death. I happen to know that it was someone else."

Mrs. Kroning resumed work on her knitting. "That don't mean nothing. I happen to know it was someone else besides me too."

"But I—I have something, a piece of paper, a note. I know it was written by the person who killed Em, and the same person must have attacked your daughter. That is—I think—" Agatha's voice died away as she realized that her suspect was Mrs. Kroning's son.

"A note? What's in it? Have you got it on you?" Mrs. Kroning asked with interest.

"It's in my room, and I shall show it to the police when the time comes."

"When what time comes?"

Agatha intended to hold onto the note until she knew for certain who had killed Em, but she was unwilling to confide as much to Mrs. Kroning. She said briefly, "It will be soon. But I wanted you to know that I did not hurt your daughter, that I could never have done such a thing."

"Between you and me and the gatepost," Mrs. Kroning said comfortably, "I believe you. Ginny is kinda wild and unsettled yet. The way she makes a bed would take the curl outa your hair. Anyways, when she wakes up I'll give her a talking to and see if I can get this thing straightened out."

Agatha nodded eagerly. "Oh yes. Please do. I'm sure she'll realize that it was not I who hit her."

"We'll see." Mrs. Kroning clicked her needles efficiently, and Agatha said that she would have to fly—there was still so much work to be done—but she would gladly bring Mrs. Kroning coffee and toast, if she liked.

Mrs. Kroning observed that she never ate between meals because it made too much of a mess, and Agatha backed out into the hall, where she came face to face with Lewis.

Lewis had been bored with the early part of the conversation, but Agatha's confidence regarding the note had made him forget both his boredom and his aching feet. Something to get his teeth into at last—a note from the murderer! The fact that Miss Bunson knew she hadn't killed Em because she had a note from the murderer was a bit puzzling, but he felt that he had the answer to it in the back of his head somewhere. The first thing was to get the note.

"Miss Bunson, I wish to speak to you privately—perhaps your room?"

"Oh no!" Agatha stared at him. Her bedroom! What was the man thinking of!

"It's either that, or I'll have to ask you to come down to police headquarters."

Agatha's face went gray, and Lewis put a steadying hand on her arm. "You must realize, Miss Bunson, that the young lady has accused you of attacking her, and I believe also that it was you who put the suitcase in the corner of the trunk room. I think you knew that Em was in that closet. So you can see that it's necessary for us to talk about these things. That's all."

Agatha moved her tongue around her dry mouth and found no words. That suitcase—she should have wiped the fingerprints off—

"We'd better go into your room, and you can tell me everything," Lewis said easily. "You'll have to give me the note you mentioned to Mrs. Kroning. It's your best chance to prove that you did not kill your cook."

He urged her along to her room and shut the door firmly behind them. "You see," he added almost carelessly, "I found the weapon, the one used on Miss Kroning, here in this room."

Chapter 24

"IT'S all wrong," Agatha whispered. "Don't you see that I couldn't have hit that girl? I slept all night—the pill—" She remembered the gun that had been used for Em, and ran to the drawer without thinking of Lewis. The box was in its place, and as her fumbling hands lifted the lid she saw that the gun was there, clean and apparently unused.

Lewis moved up behind her, his eyes snapping, and too late Agatha realized what she had done. He gave her no time to think but shot a series of rapid questions at her, and she found herself unable to cope with him. In the end she told him everything while the tears flowed over her cheeks.

He was accustomed to women weeping, and for a while he ignored her while his eyes stared absently into space. Presently, however, he patted her shoulder and said, "Hush. You don't want anybody to know about this. It's something just between the two of us. Now let me see that note, the one you told Mrs. Kroning about."

Agatha pulled it out of her shoe, where she had hidden it, and handed it over in silence.

Lewis read quickly and then gave her a little smile. "Good thing you hung onto this," he murmured. "It gives you a chance."

She looked at him with wet, hopeless eyes. "What's going to happen to me? Where are you going to take me?"

Lewis rattled change in his pockets and regarded his shoes for a moment before he raised his head. "Look, if you keep your mouth shut, really shut, I might arrange it so that I won't have to take you anywhere. But you'll have to clam up absolutely. Don't talk to anyone but me. If you think of anything else that you haven't told me, come and spill it—only not in front of anyone else."

She nodded mutely, and Lewis moved toward the door. "Wash your eyes in cold water—no need for anyone to see you like that—and keep quiet."

He went out and closed the door behind him. No telling, of course, whether she had written the note herself, or whether she had killed Em. Even if she had, she might have done it while she was walking in her sleep, and then again she might not. She'd been in too much of a stew to ask about the weapon he'd found in her room. Evidently she'd thought at first it was that gun. He patted his pocket. A wrench, with bloodstains but no fingerprints, lying under the old girl's bed. Looked as though it had been pl,anted, and in a hurry.

He glanced into the Kronings' bedroom, but Ginny was still sleeping and Mrs. Kroning frowned him out, so he went off on business of his own. He returned at lunch time and went first to the dining room, where he found Mrs. Kroning and Mirrie sitting at the table eating in silence. He gave Mrs. Kroning a hard stare and then turned abruptly and made for the front hall. He ran all the way to the second floor, thinking furiously that no one could have expected him to know the damned woman would be stupid enough to leave the girl alone.

Mr. Appely was standing at the door of the bedroom, and as Lewis thundered up he said mildly, "I hope she's all right in there. I've knocked, but there's no answer."

Lewis tried the door and found that it would not open, and Mr. Appely shook his head. "It's locked."

"Yes. I'd better—"

"I came in," Mr. Appely said in his precise voice, "with Will, you know, and I really cannot help but think that the fellow is callous. He was hungry, and he must needs eat before coming up to see how his sister is getting on."

"Mrs. Kroning is downstairs," Lewis muttered. "Perhaps she locked the door when she left."

"Do you mean that the girl is alone in there?" Mr. Appely asked in a tone of reproof.

Lewis was already heading for the stairs. "I'll ask Mrs. Kroning if she locked the door."

They went down together, and Lewis could feel his face burning. He should have arranged better protection for Ginny. One head wasn't enough for a job like this. You had to think of everything.

He went to the kitchen, where Mrs. Kroning and Agatha were clearing away, and asked abruptly, "Mrs. Kroning, did you lock your daughter in that room?"

"I certainly did. I know what I'm about, young fella. I'll fix her something to eat when I get through here—the doctor told me what she can have—and she's goin' home tomorrow, see?"

Lewis nodded and retired to the dining room.

Mirrie looked up when he came in, and they exchanged warm smiles. Will gave him a bleak eye and said coldly, "You back?"

"It looks like me."

"I suppose you got the case all buttoned up, ready to hang on the wrong guy."

"I've nothing to say just now," Lewis declared formally, "but I expect to be able to report very shortly."

"Yeah." Will rolled his toothpick to the other side of his mouth. "Report off the force, maybe."

Lewis shrugged. "Where is Mrs. Rost? I thought she usually had lunch here."

"She hasn't come in today," Allen told him. "She's often here, but not always."

"I seen her this morning," Will offered. "She give me a snort. Sez I needed it, which I did. She told me she had a date for lunch, but she ast me would I be here at dinner."

"What's it to her if you're here for dinner or not?" Mirrie asked, and picked irritably at a hangnail.

"You ain't got no reason to be jealous, baby," Will said soothingly. "The Rost babe don't cut no ice with me, but a guy can't help it if the dames fall for him."

Mirrie cried, "Will!" and blushed to the eyebrows.

Lewis grinned. "He was like that in school, all the little girls writing him notes and waiting to walk home with him. It never changed him, though. Just the same modest Will, giving each little girl a break so that no one would feel left out."

Will gave him a suspicious glare and mumbled, "Why don't you get outa here and do some work for us tax-payin' suckers?"

"Oh yes, pardon me." Lewis bowed to Mirrie and departed for the kitchen in search of Agatha. He heard Mirrie's furious "Will! Why do you have to be so *rude*?" But he was out of earshot of Will's reply.

Mrs. Kroning and Agatha were still working in the kitchen and were chatting quite amiably. Lewis waited for a break and then suggested seriously, "Shouldn't you go back to your daughter, Mrs. Kroning? She's been alone for a long time."

Mrs. Kroning turned her small hazel eyes upon him, and they were without warmth. "If you got time for other people after seein' to your own affairs, mister, don't waste none of it on me. I'm stayin' here till this kitchen is spick-and-span, after which I'll fix a tray for my daughter, after which I'll go upstairs. If that don't suit you, I don't know what you can do about it."

Lewis abandoned her and turned his attention to Agatha. "I'd like to speak to you for a moment," he said, and indicated the sitting room.

"But I can't." Agatha tried to back away from him. "I haven't time. I must finish here—"

Lewis urged her into the sitting room and closed the door, nor did he regret that the sound of its closing blotted out a loud remark flung after him by Mrs. Kroning.

"I want to know, Miss Bunson, just how much cash you brought home to Em last year, and up until now?"

"Oh dear—I—let me see." She ran a hand rather wildly over her hair. "Well, I brought cash home to her several times, quite a lot. The first time—" She paused and began a mental calculation. When she had at last arrived at a total there was a look of awe on her face. "Why, it must have been about twelve thousand dollars, at least."

Lewis nodded. "How much of it did she return to you to invest for her?"

"None of it."

"Did she tell you she was investing it herself?"

"No."

"How did she get as much money as that?"

"But I told you," Agatha said vaguely. "Em didn't spend anything, much. She saved her money."

Lewis shook his head. "She never saved that amount. Perhaps your father gave her some?"

"Oh no," Agatha said in a shocked voice. "Why would he? He paid her decent wages. It would be absurd."

Lewis reflected that if Em had gouged any money from the doctor, Agatha wouldn't be the type to know about it anyway. He said, "All right. Thank you," and allowed her to escape back to the kitchen.

He went out into the hall and picked up Mr. Appely, who was emerging from the dining room. He backed him against the wall, where they were out of sight of Christine's doorway.

"Did this Em lend money to anyone besides yourself?" he asked.

Mr. Appely's prim little face lengthened, and he spoke reluctantly. "Why, she—I believe she did lend some around, yes. It's hardly my place to mention it, however, and I'm sure it's perfectly all right—"

"Did she lend some to Mrs. Rost?"

Mr. Appely traced a pattern on the carpet with the toe of his shoe and murmured, "Well, er, I really don't—"

"Did she?"

Mr. Appely drew a long breath and said bravely, "Yes."

"How much?"

"Well, as to that, I don't—I mean, I'm not—"

"Mrs. Rost must have it on her books," Lewis said patiently, "so there's no point in your not telling me."

"No, I—I suppose not. As far as I know, she borrowed somewhat more than I did, about five thousand, I believe."

"Did she get it at the same time as you got yours?"

"No, no. About a month or so later. That's why she has not come with her interest check, you see. It would not be due for another month."

Lewis let him go and watched him scurry out the front door, and then he went back to the kitchen.

Mrs. Kroning had been arranging a tray, and as he came in she picked it up, but she had her back to him and did not see him. "I'll be back in a minute, Agatha," she called over her shoulder. "We'll pitch into that fretwork in the dining room. We can finish it if we just keep goin', and that stoopid ape of a cop don't interrupt."

Agatha looked almost happy, Lewis thought, and there was a lilt in her voice as she replied, "All right, Mabel. I'll have everything ready."

She turned and saw Lewis, and her face pinched in again. He passed her by, however, with only a fleeting smile and went on up the back stairs. He found Mrs. Kroning trying to unlock Ginny's door with one hand while she balanced the tray precariously on the other, and he took the tray from her immediately. As she fitted the key into the lock he said, "You and Miss Bunson seem to know each other pretty well. Did you often visit together?"

"Never met her before," Mrs. Kroning replied shortly, without looking at him. "Heard plenty about her, just the sort of nasty things them gossips always hand out, and not a word of it true. She's a nice, decent lady."

"I think so too," Lewis agreed absently. He followed her into the room and glanced quickly at the bed. Ginny appeared to be sleeping peacefully, and, reassured, he asked Mrs. Kroning, "Do you think she was mistaken when she accused Miss Bunson of hitting her?"

Mrs. Kroning took the tray from him and put it on a table by the bed. She let a moment pass before she said carelessly, "Oh, Ginny's always jumpin' to conclusions, and anyways, she fibs as easy as she breathes."

She shook the girl's shoulder, and Lewis said uneasily, "Do you think you ought to do that?"

Mrs. Kroning ignored him. "Come on, Ginny, wake up now. I got some lunch for you. You don't want to let it get cold."

Ginny opened her eyes, and Mrs. Kroning hauled her into a sitting position and thrust pillows behind her. She placed the tray on her lap and said, "Eat it up like a good girl, after I broke my back fixin' it for you."

Ginny looked at the tray vaguely and her eyelids drooped. "That all I get? Stingy!"

"I'm doin' what the doctor told me," Mrs. Kroning said severely. "You'll maybe get more for dinner."

Ginny leaned back against the pillows and moaned, "Oh, my goddamned head!"

"You watch your language, and eat your lunch."

The girl opened and closed her eyes once or twice, and then began to pick at the food in front of her.

Lewis drew Mrs. Kroning away from the bed and asked in a low voice, "Can you tell me where Em got all that money? Did

Miss Bunson's father give it to her?"

Unexpectedly Mrs. Kroning blushed up to the roots of her hair. She folded her lips into a thin line and then opened them to say, "I know nothin' about how much money the doctor gave Em."

Lewis was silent for a moment while he absorbed the blush, and then he said easily, "But of course there was a reason for the doctor having given Em money over and above her salary."

"Mr. Lewis," said Mrs. Kroning firmly, "I never been one to gossip."

"No, of course not. I realize that. I wouldn't ask you now, except for the fact that I'm trying to catch a murderer."

"Ahh, I don't think Em was murdered. Likely she went into that closet to count over her money and hit her head. She was always sloppy in her ways, that one. Ginny hit her head the same way, tryin' to get in there and snoop, is what I think, and that's all there is to it."

Lewis had more to say, but she gave him short shrift. He'd have to go now. She had things to do for her patient and she didn't want him underfoot, not to mention the fact that it was highly indelicate for him to be hanging around in a lady's bedroom, anyways.

He went slowly down the stairs and came upon Christine heading for her apartment. He asked if he could speak to her, and she nodded and led him inside.

They sat down, and Lewis said directly, "I don't suppose you'd know why Mrs. Kroning should blush when I asked her whether Miss Bunson's father had supplied some of Em's money?"

Christine hesitated and then laughed. "I suppose I ought to tell you, really. It seems that Ginny is Em's daughter, and perhaps the doctor was her father."

Lewis said slowly, "Yes. That would explain it. Where did you get this information?"

Christine told him, and he stood up. "I'll go and speak to Dr. Gremson."

Fred Slupp was in the hall, and as Lewis came out he whirled around, waving a fistful of currency.

"It's using my cellar they are, all the time, to hide their greedy gains and other things, and I'll not put up with it."

Chapter 25

LEWIS urged Fred into the kitchen and demanded crossly, "Why do you have to go screaming into the hall with that stuff?"

"I thought Miss Agatha was out there at her cleaning. It's her day to be out there at the woodwork and all, and how in the name of God was I to know that she'd taken her pots and pans elsewhere?"

"Where did you find all this money?" Lewis asked impatiently.

"It's in the icebox I found it, and I want to hand it over to Miss Agatha."

Lewis glanced across the kitchen. "You mean in the refrigerator there?"

Fred shook his head peevishly. "I mean the old icebox in the cellar, the same that the doctor had carted down there when he bought this thing that runs on electricity and its own whims."

"Oh." Lewis nodded. "How'd you come to find it in a place like that?"

"I was cleaning the thing in the line of me regular duty."

"You keep more food down there?"

"We do not. The old doctor was never one to skimp, and there's room and to spare up here for all the food."

"What's it used for then?"

"Nothing."

Lewis heaved an exasperated little sigh, but he asked patiently enough, "Why do you clean it if it's never used?"

"It's me duty to keep the cellar clean and I'll not shirk it. Once a week I dust the outside of the old box and once a month I go inside with me rags." He glanced down at the money which was still clutched in his hand. "This was in the top where the ice used to go."

"I'll take charge of it," Lewis said.

"You'll not." Fred put his hand behind his back. "Miss Agatha owns the house here, and I'll give it to her."

"O.K.," Lewis said easily, "we'll go up and find her now."

Agatha was busy in the doctor's room, but she stopped her labors and pushed straying hair back from her face. She seemed genuinely surprised at the sight of the money, and Lewis watched her as she counted it. The sum was short of five thousand by a few dollars, and it was mostly in hundred-dollar bills.

"Do you think this is Em's money?" Lewis asked.

Agatha looked down at it. "Yes, but she used to keep it in a paper bag, you know."

"There was no paper bag, miss," Fred declared. "Loose, it was, in the old icebox in the cellar."

"But—" Agatha looked at them. "Em never went near the cellar."

"No," Fred said emphatically.

"Why not?" Lewis asked.

"Well—" Agatha hesitated. "She complained that there were too many stairs, but it wasn't that."

Fred said, "No."

"What was it then?"

"She was afraid," Agatha sighed.

"Yes?"

"Yes," said Fred.

"Afraid of what?"

Agatha shrugged. "She always said that there was something evil down there."

"Didn't she say what it was?"

Agatha shook her head. "No, that was all. Just something evil. I asked her once what it was, but she said that it was nothing to concern Fred or myself. The evil was all for her."

"Are you quite sure that she never went down there?"

"Quite sure. I didn't pay much attention to it because she was so superstitious, always talking about ghosts and how she communicated with the spirits."

"Did she ever speak of being in communication with your father after he had died?"

Fred nodded. "That she did."

Agatha frowned at him. "She said she did, but it always annoyed me. She had no right to bring my dead father's name into her stupid games."

Lewis was silent for a moment, and then he asked, "When you brought cash to her, was it usually in hundred-dollar bills?"

"Yes."

"Do you know what bank Mrs. Rost deals with?"

Agatha stared at him, confused by the abrupt change of subject. He repeated the question, and she said vaguely that she was sure she didn't know.

Fred added that he didn't know either and went on to ask, "What would the woman's bank be having to do with all of this?"

Agatha turned on him and said sharply, "That will do, Fred. Go on back to your work."

"And wouldn't I like to be doing me work in peace, but I no

sooner start than this one and that one is bothering the life out of me." He turned toward the door and then stopped. "Why wouldn't you be doing the front hall today, miss? This being the day for it, and all."

Agatha pressed a fist against the worried frown of her forehead. "I don't know. I'm mixed up, with all this going on—"

Fred nodded and went off, and Lewis took the money from her. "The police will keep this for the time being." He put it away with great care and added wistfully, "I don't know who'll get it in the end."

He left Agatha and went off to dispose of the money. When he returned, he went straight to Julia's interior-decorating establishment and was gratified to find her in, and alone. He asked her directly if she had borrowed five thousand dollars from Em.

She denied it hotly, and indignantly demanded the name of the person who had given such false information.

Lewis supplied it, and after a moment of obvious surprise she banged her fist on a nearby table. "The miserable little drip! I hate these mean creeps! Just because he sneaked around and borrowed money from Em he wants someone in the same boat with him."

"What is the name of your bank, Mrs. Rost?"

"Oh." Julia gave him a level look. "You want to check up on me. Sure, go ahead."

She gave him the name of the bank, told him where it was, and then asked if he'd be good enough to put her name down on Agatha's pad for dinner. "I hadn't planned to dine there tonight," she explained, "but I'd like a word with Louse Appely."

Lewis promised with the utmost courtesy to attend to it, and departed hastily. He feared that Julia's wrath would be upon his own head if she discovered that he had picked up a specimen of her handwriting. It was only a brief note from the pad by the telephone and it read, "Phone Mrs. Anderson tomorrow at ten." Lewis hoped she wouldn't forget.

He felt pleased with himself. He had handwriting specimens from all of them now except Ginny and Mrs. Kroning. He hurried back to his car and made off for the handwriting expert.

Mirrie saw him go and tossed her curls. He hadn't given her much attention today, not like he had yesterday, anyhow. But then he was busy, of course, and a man had to attend to his job. She pretended to straighten the curtains and switched her white uniform back to the desk. Sometimes, she thought, this job really got her down. Same old patients creaking around and coughing behind magazines. Anyway, Will would have money now, and he sure was gone on her, even though that redheaded old hag, Julia, was trying to wrap him up. She sniffed loudly and was immediately conscious of the fact that all the patients were looking at her. She divided a haughty stare among them and then dropped her eyes to the appointment book on her desk.

They finished early that afternoon, and Allen came out and said, "Why don't you run along? That was an inspiration, sending some of the patients over to Dr. Herser. I feel downright leisurely for a change."

Mirrie's smooth forehead puckered a little. "But I never heard of a doctor giving away patients before."

"It was only a loan," he said, smiling at her. "They'll be back here wearing out my upholstery the next time they want their toenails trimmed."

"Well—" Mirrie shook her blond head. "Maybe they felt that they just weren't important enough for you to bother with, and you know patients don't like that, even though it is only toenails."

He gave a laugh that ended in a yawn, nodded to her, and disappeared into the hall. Mirrie went to the small lavatory where she always changed her clothes and decided that she was not going to tire herself by hunting for Will. Let him call her up at her home. She needed a little rest.

Lewis had managed a short sleep for himself and had been awakened by the handwriting expert who bore the note Agatha had found under her pillow and Mr. Appely's I.O.U. for three thousand dollars.

"These are the same."

Lewis shook the sleep from his head and stood up. "Mr. Appely?" he murmured.

"Not the signature. The writing at the top."

Lewis stared down at the note. "I.O.U. three thousand dollars and agree to pay five per cent interest on it every six months." Mr. Appely's signature beneath was not in the same handwriting.

"But this is impossible," Lewis muttered. "It's Em's handwriting."

Chapter 26

LEWIS went to a diner for a cup of coffee, but his thoughts were far away. Em couldn't have written that note. He'd had a report on her, and she'd been dead for too long, unless there could have been some mistake in the report. Agatha had heard the chair rocking in there. No. She'd imagined it, or else Em's body had just fallen to the floor, and the chair had rocked for a moment when Agatha happened to be passing. That was it, of course. So who had written the note?

He finished his coffee and drove back to the house. A brief search for Agatha brought him to the kitchen, where she was busy cooking the dinner, and he remembered to tell her that Julia was coming in. He added that she had better lock the front and back doors after dinner if the doctors were not having evening office hours.

Agatha gave him a brief nod which indicated as much impatience as she dared to show. He turned away, and she fumed quietly as she heard him mount the back stairs. What right had he to make himself at home this way? Tracking dirt all over her clean house and annoying people. She was helpless to do anything about it, though. She'd told him everything, and he might decide at any minute to drag her off to some wretched, filthy place where she wouldn't be allowed to keep things clean around her.

Mrs. Kroning walked into the kitchen and looked around for an apron, and Agatha gave a little sigh of relief. It was so hard to do the cooking all by herself when she couldn't keep her mind on things.

"What's that guy Lewis still hanging around for?" Mrs. Kroning asked.

Agatha twisted her hands. "I can't help it. I can't do anything about it. He—he has to find out what happened to Em."

"I told him what happened to Em," Mrs. Kroning said sharply. "She bumped her head on the back side of the stairs, snooping in that closet, and so did Ginny."

Agatha was comforted against reason, and they went to work on the dinner with a harmonious exchange of idle talk.

On the second floor Lewis was collecting keys from the various doors. He had assumed correctly that Mrs. Kroning had the key to Ginny's room in her pocket, and he brought his collection to the door and began to try them, one after the other. He was unsuccessful, and became a little rattled when the girl's voice called, "Hey, Ma! That you? What in hell are you doin'?"

Lewis went to the third floor for more keys and eventually tried one that fitted. He found Ginny half sitting up in bed and asked politely, "How are you feeling, Miss Kroning?"

"O.K., I guess. Who are you, anyways?"

"My name is Lewis. I'm afraid I've disturbed you, but your

mother asked me to look in on you, and I had a little trouble opening the door. Mrs. Kroning is downstairs helping Miss Bunson with the dinner."

"No kiddin'?" Ginny shook her head at the vagaries of her mother's temperament. "I hope she don't turn her back on the old bat once too often. She's liable to get brained with a frying pan."

"Are you sure it was Miss Bunson who hit you?" Lewis asked.

"Sure, I'm sure."

"Where were you?"

"I was right down in the back hall there, lookin' for Em," Ginny told him with some heat, "and that old bag of bones comes up behind and smacks me one."

"Did you see her face to face?"

"Huh?"

"Were you facing her when she hit you?"

"I already told you," Ginny said impatiently. "She come up behind me."

"Then how can you be sure it was Miss Bunson?"

"Who in hell else could it be?"

Lewis shook his head. "Actually, you don't know who hit you, do you? It's a very serious thing to make an idle accusation like that."

"Oh, put it in your hat!" Ginny said, and kicked at the bed-clothes. "I know it was her, and I'm sayin' so."

"Why did you come here in the first place?"

"I told you that too. I was lookin' for Em. Will phoned out to the house about it, and I thought maybe I could find her."

"You came in late last night?"

"Well, sure. See, Ma raised a stink about me comin', so I hadda wait till after dinner before I could sneak out. I left Ma a note."

"When you arrived here you walked in the front door and went straight upstairs?"

"Yep."

"Where did you go after you got to the second floor?"

"For chrissake!" Ginny said in a tone of mild exasperation. "You gonna stand there all night astin' whatever comes into your head?"

Lewis became a little severe. "I must know these things. It's my job to find out what happened to your aunt."

"So what? I don't know nothin' about it."

"You might," said Lewis, "have seen something that could help me. What did you do after you came up to the second floor?"

Ginny sighed. "I went up to Em's room, and when I seen she

wasn't there I come on down to the kitchen. She wasn't there neither, so I went into that hall in the back, and then that loony old crow sneaked up behind me with a baseball bat, or something."

Lewis nodded with reserve. The girl's hands were restless on the bedclothes, and he thought that something was bothering her. He was about to try to probe for it when Christine walked into the room and gave him a rather austere, professional glance, and he backed away in faint confusion.

Christine went briskly to the bed, and Lewis retired to the farthest corner of the room, where he was partly concealed by the end of a bureau. He watched and listened in silence while Christine attended to her patient, and pressed closer into his corner when Allen walked into the room.

"How is she?" Allen asked.

Ginny gave him an appraising look, and her hand strayed to her hair. "I'm O.K., brother. Where's Ma?"

"Downstairs with Miss Bunson."

"Yeah? Havin' a swell time raking over all the dirt, huh? And the hell with Em."

"Oh no," Christine said, "that isn't fair. You lie quietly now. Your mother will be up presently."

"I been lyin' quiet too long already. I got corns on my fanny. I'm gonna get up."

"No." Christine put a hand on her shoulder. "Not until tomorrow."

Ginny raised an eyebrow at Allen. "You ride along with that, brother?"

"Certainly do."

"O.K. Then will you kindly get the hell outa here while I try to get some stinkin' sleep which I don't want?"

Christine and Allen went downstairs together. "I've been looking for you," he told her. "Lewis has the doors locked, with all of us inside. Even Mirrie is back. Seems he phoned her and asked her to dine with him here tonight, but she's down there with Will just now. Julia is in your rooms, waiting for us to join her in a cocktail."

Christine nodded. "Fine. You go and kiss her or something while I finish up with my last patient."

"I won't kiss her or something. Who's your last patient?"

"Agatha."

"There's nothing wrong with Agatha. She's jabbering with her new friend, who seems to be called Mabel, and I don't think she'd welcome an interruption, or want to pay for it."

"I merely want to look at her face," Christine said coldly.

"And I don't intend to put it on her bill. She changes moods so often."

Allen followed her into the kitchen, and they found Mrs. Kroning stirring something in a saucepan while Agatha wiped off a table. Her head jerked up as Christine came in, and there was a startled look in her eyes.

"Oh, er—I just wondered—" Christine's tone was entirely casual. "Is there an evening paper in the house?"

Agatha dropped her cloth, and her hands fastened together.

"Miss Bunson is busy. I have an evening paper. Come on." Allen turned Christine firmly around and steered her into the hall. "You see? As I said, she doesn't want to be disturbed."

Julia was waiting for them with a cocktail in one hand and a cigarette in the other, and she looked depressed. "Lord, I'm glad to see you. I've been thinking about taking an overdose of my sleeping pills."

"Pour me a cocktail first," Christine said, dropping into a chair. "Why do you want to make work for the undertaker?"

"Shut up, will you? It's a bunch of so-called painters. They've put on the wrong color."

"Impossible?" Allen asked.

"Quite impossible."

"No, it isn't." Christine stretched out in her chair. "No color is the wrong color, unless it's put with the wrong things."

Julia was silent for a moment, her eyes on Christine, and then she gave a little laugh. "Damned if you don't have something there. I can change the coloring of the other things. I'm lucky on this job. They've given me my head."

"What's this business about our being locked in?" Christine asked.

"I think our Mr. Lewis has something up his sleeve," Allen said thoughtfully. "He's collecting the keys to the front and back doors and to the cellar door that leads into the back yard. Promises to let anyone out who wants to go. But I still think there was something more to his asking Mirrie here than the lure of her blond charms."

Julia extended her glass. "Refill, please. If you ask me, I think he has a nerve. He'll let me out after dinner or I'll show him what happens when red-haired women get a little vexed."

"It seems to me that anyone could get in or out of the windows on the ground floor," Christine suggested.

"Well—" Allen shrugged. "They'd have to use a ladder. There's a high cellar here."

"Where's Mirrie?" Julia asked.

"She's over in my waiting room with Will."

"Oh, he's here? Well, go over and invite them for cocktails. I brought a whole mix."

"Do you want them?" Allen said reluctantly.

"Sure, why not? Don't be so stingy."

Mirrie, appearing shortly thereafter with Will, was both pleased and suspicious. She liked being included in this intimate little cocktail party, but she rightly suspected that Julia merely wished to while away some time with Will.

Julia moved in at once. Will responded with raucous banter, and Christine and Allen laughed, while Mirrie went into a slow burn.

The noise was at its height when the door flew open, and Ginny walked in clad only in her pajamas. She sprayed them with a wild look and then turned to Will.

"Hey, listen! I gotta get out of here! I just heard that Lewis guy tellin' Mr. Appely he knows I killed Em."

Chapter 27

CHRISTINE and Allen moved forward together, and Ginny was presently stretched upon the couch with a blanket over her.

She kicked it off irritably. "I'm too hot, anyways, and I want to get outa here. That creep's tryin' to frame me, and he'll lock me up if I don't make a getaway."

"You're being absurd," Christine said calmly. "Lewis was just talking, trying to get a reaction, perhaps. Anyway, you'll be safe here."

"What did Mr. Appely say?" Julia asked. "Did he defend you, or throw you to the wolves?"

Ginny bushed and muttered, "He didn't say nothin'. He coulda stood up for me, the louse."

"Don't pay no attention to that little Appely," Will told her. "He's been tryin' to get rid of his shadow for years because it keeps following him. And I'm gonna fix Lewis. The slob is gettin' too big for his britches. He musta paid big dough, which he stole offa somebody, to get promoted off the beat. Now you stay here and take it easy, kid. I'm gonna find that monkey right now and twist his snoopin' nose off his face."

He left, apparently unconscious of Mirrie's restraining hand, and began a fruitless search which eventually landed him in the kitchen. Mrs. Kroning was there, comfortably busy, and Will slowed to a stop.

"Wotcha doin' here, Ma?"

Mrs. Kroning turned the gas low under a saucepan and regarded him with her hands on her hips. "What do I look like I was doin'? Pickin' daisies?"

"Well, wot're you down here cookin' for?" Will demanded. "Ain'tcha supposed to be lookin' after Ginny?"

Mrs. Kroning's eyes narrowed. "You mind your own business, Will Kroning, and I'll tend to mine. I'm lookin' after Ginny by gettin' her a meal she can eat, and me too. I got to keep my strength up for this job."

Will knew his mother well enough to change his tone at this point. He became conciliatory. "Well, sure, Ma, but I wished you woulda called me when you hadda leave her. Here she's racin' all over the house with her hair flyin' in the wind because that stinkin' Lewis made a crack about her."

Mrs. Kroning dropped a spoon, which clattered to the floor, and yelled, "What are you talkin' about."

Agatha had not digested the slurs cast on her cooking. She hurried over, retrieved the spoon, washed and dried it, and handed it back to Mrs. Kroning.

"I'm tryin' to tell you, ain't I?" Will said. "Ginny ain't where you left her. She's out front in that Herser dame's room. And I'm lookin' for that guy Lewis. Where is he?"

"How should I know where he is? As for Ginny, I left her sleepin', and I locked the door and here's the key. See?"

Will discarded appeasement and spoke in anger. "Ain'tcha got no sense, Ma? That thing's a skeleton key. Any old key will do for a lock like that. Somebody picked up another key and got in. She mighta been killed. That's how the door's open. The murderer musta been scared off—that dopey ape, Lewis, talkin' to Mr. Appely—so he skipped, and Ginny heard him and got scared. I want to get my hands on him. Where in hell is he?"

"I can't make head nor tail to what you're sayin'," Mrs. Kroning declared, but she looked for the first time genuinely uneasy. Agatha was gazing at them with a puzzled expression.

"I ain't got time to draw you a picture," Will said crossly. "Just remember, when you lock Ginny in with a key like that, you ain't got her locked in at all, see?"

Mrs. Kroning wiped her hands on her apron and started to untie it, but Will stretched a restraining arm.

"There ain't no use dumpin' the dinner now you got it started.

I gotta eat soon or I'll cave in. I'll look out for Ginny until you get through."

Mrs. Kroning hesitated and then turned to the stove. "What's she doin' runnin' all over the house, anyways? If that girl don't stop her flighty ways, she'll end up in trouble." She banged a lid onto a pot and added, "Dinner's just about ready, and no thanks to you, Will Kroning, bustin' in here and givin' me sass when I'm in the middle of it."

Will was peering into the little sitting room, and he muttered, "Where *is* that lousy dick?"

Agatha worried up behind him. "Please, there's no one in there, no one at all. If you want Mr. Lewis, you'll surely see him at dinner. He's invited that nurse of Dr. Gremson's. He'll pay for her. I think he must be interested. He wrote both their names on the pad, but I wish he'd take her out instead."

Will's face darkened and seemed to swell. He whispered, "That dirty bastard!"

"You keep your saloon talk out of this decent kitchen," Mrs. Kroning said severely.

Will ignored her and put his face close to Agatha's. "You don't *never* take no money from that guy for her, see? *I'm* the guy's payin' for Mirrie, and the *only* guy. Get it?"

Agatha got it and accompanied her nod with an audible sniff. She had known that he would be infuriated, but she had wanted to divert him from poking into her sitting room.

Mrs. Kroning removed her apron. "Will, get Ginny back upstairs and come eat yourself. Agatha, ring the gong. I'm all set and I don't want things spoiled. And, Will, you tell Ginny to stay put this time, or she'll hear from me."

Will was already pounding along the hall, still stewing over Lewis's intention to pay for Mirrie's dinner. He flung open Christine's door without knocking and was immediately diverted by the sight of Ginny sitting up with a highball in her hand.

"Hey! What's goin' on here? What in hell do you think you're doin', gettin' stewed in your condition?"

Ginny gave him a cold eye. "You're talkin'? I suppose they didn't wheel you up to the operatin' room to snatch your tonsils, and you singin' 'Work for the Night Is Comin' ' at the top of your foghorn voice?"

Will blushed and said weakly, "Shut your trap or I'll shut it for you."

Ginny had expressed fear at being left alone, and Christine, uneasy herself, decided that she could go to the dining room with them. They escorted her in and seated her carefully, and

Agatha began to wring her hands at once. No place had been set. They were not prepared— Mrs. Kroning frowned and said that she was cooking something special for Ginny. She shouldn't be eating a heavy meal like this.

"You need not worry about that, Mrs. Kroning," Allen said, "as long as Ginny's doctor approves."

Mrs. Kroning was not soothed. "No doctor is gonna tell me what that kid should or shouldn't eat. I been feeding her enough years, and I know what's good for her, see?"

Christine and Allen masked their faces, and Will muttered, "Chrissake, Ma! Mind your manners."

Mr. Appely came in and Will, who had just seated Mirrie beside himself, eagerly indicated the chair on her other side. But Mr. Appely had been sunk in routine for a good many years, and he took his usual place at the end of the table, facing Agatha. He sent a glance around and murmured, "Good evening."

Ginny scowled at him. "I heard that fella tellin' you I killed Em, and not a word outa you, though you know I wasn't even here."

Mr. Appely gave her a steady look, and she flushed and dropped her eyes. "My dear young lady, it would take a more verbose man than myself to tell Inspector Lewis anything. It is he who does the talking."

Will gave a guffaw which ended in a belch and said, "Pardon me."

Mirrie turned a little away from him. "Where is Inspector Lewis? I would have stayed home tonight, but he insisted on dating me."

"*He* ain't dating you. *I* am," Will informed her loudly. "Any time he gets in your hair, just give him the brush. Tell him I got an option every night."

Julia leaned back in her chair and laughed. "Why, I think that's wonderful. Aren't you flattered, Mirrie?"

Will expanded his chest and grinned broadly, and he and Julia fell into a lively run of chatter. Mirrie began to burn again until Lewis slipped quietly into the chair beside her and apologized in a low voice for being late. Mirrie gave him a charming smile and was annoyed because Will hadn't noticed him. Will paid too much attention to food, anyway, she thought angrily, and maybe he was putting on an extra act now just because his mother had cooked the stuff.

Julia had quieted down too. She was aware of Lewis and gave him a venomous glance. Well, at least he wouldn't have found anything at the bank. She had used the money for cash expenses.

He probably figured it that way, though, and she was uneasy. She felt a little shiver creep along her spine and turned her eyes to Mr. Appely. The edge of her temper had worn off, but just the same she would get even with him for opening his nasty prim mouth.

Will raised his head from his plate for a moment and noticed Lewis. He acted promptly, without taking time for words. Almost in one movement he pushed his chair back, swung Mirrie and her chair down to his place, and seated himself where she had been.

Lewis said, "Quite frankly, I don't find you a pleasant substitute for Miss Mirrie."

"Why don'tcha leave them fancy words in the ditchanary?" Will asked coldly. "Where they look much better than comin' outa your fat face. I heard how you been tryin' to make time with my girl behind my back."

"Are you engaged?"

"We're goin' steady, Stinky, so paste that in your hat where you won't forget it."

Mirrie said, "Will! Please!" from the depths of her embarrassment.

Julia laughed, and Mr. Appely chimed in until he caught her eye, when he looked away hastily.

"Mr. Lewis," Julia said peremptorily, "did you check with my bank and discover that I did not borrow money from Em?"

Lewis gave her a faintly reproving glance and made no reply, and Mr. Appely coughed and devoted himself to his plate.

"I cannot understand," Julia went on coldly, "why Mr. Appely should have said that I did. Perhaps he didn't want it thought that he was the only one who crept around and borrowed money from a cook."

"She was not a cook!" Ginny yelled suddenly. "She was housekeeper here, see? When the doctor was alive everybody knew she was housekeeper, only since he croaked that old bat daughter of his tried to make Em into a cook."

Mr. Appely nodded and cleared his throat. "That is quite true. In the doctor's time Em was housekeeper, and, I believe, had her meals at the table with the family."

"She never did!" Agatha cried in a high voice. "Not *ever!*"

Lewis stirred and looked up. "That seems odd—because she was your father's wife."

Chapter 28

IN THE dead silence that followed Lewis's announcement Agatha struggled up from her chair. She held onto the table with one rigid hand and her blue lips moved a little, but she was unable to produce any sound.

Christine got up and moved quickly to her side. "Face it squarely, Miss Bunson, and you'll see that it's nothing. It doesn't really matter, you know."

Agatha drew a long breath and released her hold on the table. She said simply, "It's a lie."

"Then why did she want to keep me a secret for?" Ginny cried shrilly.

Agatha turned to her and whispered, "You? Oh no!"

"Sure thing. And here all my life I hadda keep it under my hat."

"I thought Will was Em's favorite," Julia said wonderingly.

Ginny began to cry and, having no handkerchief, mopped at her tears with her sleeve. "He was her favorite, all right, and me her own daughter, but she always liked him best."

"Cut it out, kid," Will said uncomfortably. "Ma feels about you like you was her own, and me too. Em never seen us much."

Mrs. Kroning extended a clean handkerchief and said, "Blow your nose, Ginny, and stop your nonsense. You and Will and me are all of a piece, and Em don't mean any more to you than she does to us. Leave her rest, wherever she is."

"Yeah, well—— Ginny gave a loud sniffle and her tears ceased to flow. "I guess it don't matter."

Lewis said, "Mr. Appely, suppose you tell us why the doctor kept his wife and daughter a secret."

Mr. Appely frowned, and the color rose in his face. "My dear sir, I don't see why you think that I—"

"Before you really get into it," Lewis interrupted, "you might as well know that Ginny was overheard talking to Mrs. Kroning about being Em's daughter. As soon as I learned of it I looked up records of marriages at around that time and found what I was after. You were one of the witnesses."

Mr. Appely appeared to be in acute distress. He fumbled with his napkin, dropped a fork to the floor, and murmured, "Well,

138

I—yes, I went along. A—a favor to the doctor, you see. I was merely a patient of his at the time, and he didn't want his friends to know."

"Why did he marry her?" Lewis asked. "You must know that."

Mr. Appely looked as though he would deny it, but a hasty glance at Lewis's face changed his mind. He blushed out to the ends of his prominent ears but said bravely, "I believe he thought he might be going to have a son—he had always wanted a boy most desperately. When the—er—baby proved to be a girl, he would have nothing to do with it. I gathered that Em put up with all this because of the money he gave her to keep quiet. He paid her regularly, but he would have nothing to do with her either after the baby was born."

"After his death, Em could have claimed her share of his estate," Lewis mused.

Agatha said dully, "That explains it. There was no money, just the house, nothing but what was in his account at the time. He'd sold all the land around the house. Nothing was left."

Mr. Appely folded his napkin and rose. "If you will excuse me—"

Lewis swung around. "Just a minute. I'm interested in how well you know Miss Ginny."

"Mr. Lewis! There really are limits! I do not—I mean, I hardly—"

"I found her purse in your room, on a chair, where she must have left it. I assume that she visited you last night and forgot it when she left."

Ginny flashed scornful eyes at Mr. Appely's stricken face. "The old goat! He wanted to marry me, see? I guess he knew Em hadda hatful of money, and he musta knew she was my mother too. Why, the lousy bastard!"

Mrs. Kroning rapped sharply on the table and said, "Don't talk so common!"

Mr. Appely spoke at the same time, and was eventually heard to be saying that this was all the thanks he got for his disinterested kindness to an unfortunate child. He added that he had never asked Ginny to marry him at any time, and left the room before anyone could stop him.

Ginny flung a noun and a qualifying adjective after him, which brought Mrs. Kroning to her feet. "You ain't too old to have your mouth washed out with soap, and I mean it. Hear me?"

Ginny subsided at once. "O.K., Ma, but he *did* try to get me to marry him, and him old enough to be my father."

Julia squirmed happily in her chair. "My God, I'm glad I came tonight! I wouldn't have missed this for a kingdom."

"You women and your gossip," Will said tolerantly.

Julia ignored him, and Mirrie was immediately on the alert. Why was the conceited hag giving him the cold shoulder all of a sudden? Did it mean that Will would get none of Em's money?

Agatha said faintly, "I'm afraid I shall have to go and lie down. I never dreamed that my father—that— Oh, I knew he went out with women—disgraceful—sometimes he even brought them here."

"Aggie!" Mrs. Kroning put a firm hand on Agatha's arm and pushed her back into her chair. "You sit right there and eat your dinner. You haven't touched a thing. You have a lot to learn about men if you pass up good food just because you hear one of them acted natural. You can't lay down now, anyways. We have the dishes to do and your father's didos ain't goin' to interfere with them."

Agatha sat down like an obedient child and began to pick at the food on her plate.

Will leaned back in his chair and loosened his belt. "It's like I always say about those good little guys that don't have no fun, they gotta bust out somewheres, and nine times outa ten they bust out mean. That stinkin' little Appely, sellin' greetin' cards with pretty flowers all over them like butter wouldn't melt in his mouth, and then sneakin' around our Ginny tryin' to get money offa her. I coulda told him Em left most of her money to me. I seen her will. I ain't cheap, though, and I'll do what's right. We'll divvy three ways, huh, Ma? You and me and Ginny." He paused to laugh and added, "Gee, Ma, Em would turn over in her grave, when she gets there, if she knew you was gonna get some of her money."

Mirrie's hands folded into small fists in her lap, and she wondered how she could possibly stop him from handing money around like that.

Mrs. Kroning said, "Hush! Don't never speak disrespectful of the dead."

"O.K." Will grinned at her. "Listen, ain'tcha got some pies out there? And how about some hot corfee?"

Mrs. Kroning nodded and went out to the kitchen, and Agatha thankfully abandoned her food and began to gather up plates. Christine started up to help her but was pulled back into her chair again by Allen, who whispered, "Do you want to lose prestige? Doctors always pretend that they're above housework."

"She's bad again," Christine muttered. "That information about her father—she's tight as a drum."

"You're spending too much time on her head. You're not a psychiatrist. I suppose if she cut her finger off, you'd shove some sticking plaster on the stump and start trying to find out what made her absentminded enough to do it."

"Maybe that would help her more than the beautiful-looking stump you'd fix up for her," Christine retorted. "And maybe it would keep her from getting another stump sometime too."

Julia blew cigarette smoke toward the ceiling. "Now that things have quieted down I'm getting bored. Do you two have to whisper your secrets so that I can't hear them?"

Will and Mirrie were talking together in low tones and occasionally at the same time. Will was darkly troubled about baseball. His team had made what he considered a bad trade, and despite all this upset with Ginny and Em, he hadn't been able to shake it from his mind. Mirrie was complaining about how badly her mother treated her at home, and now, what with all the scandal here, Mother might forbid her to work in the house any longer.

Lewis was thinking that Ginny looked tired and should be back in bed. Not that it was his place to say anything. It was up to the doctor. But you couldn't tell doctors anything these days, not even your own symptoms. There was nothing, he reflected gloomily, that bored a doctor like symptoms.

He looked across at Ginny and asked, "How did you come to meet Mr. Appely?"

Ginny shrugged. "He wrote me a letter and said any time I was in town he'd like to take me to dinner. Said he seen a picture Em had of me."

"So you got in touch with him when you next came to town?"

"I came a purpose, but I sure was disappointed when I seen him, so old and all. Anyways, he took me around some and it was kinda fun. Ma didn't know. She's awful proper and she wouldn't allowed it, so I couldn't get in often, and he wouldn't let me come here any time. I always hadda meet him outside his shop. Once after he put me on the bus I got off and followed him home. I thought I'd drop in on Em. I knew she was my mother, and she never came to see us no more. Anyways, I followed him and seen him go into his room, and I went on up to the attic and had a visit with Em. Pretty soon she sez come on down to the kitchen for corfee, so on the second floor we run smack into Appely. Right away he pretends he don't know me, and Em says, 'This is my niece,' and he says, 'Glad to know you' or something. It made me sore, and I didn't come in again for a while, but he kept writin' letters beggin' me to see him, so at last I did. I told him why I was sore, and he said he was sorry and all like that. Said he didn't want to embarrass me in front of Em."

Lewis assumed a shocked look and put sympathy into his

voice. "When did he ask you to marry him?"

"Just this here last week. Sent me a letter and said he couldn't live without me no more. Got me all lathered up, see? I kind of thought it might be nice to live in town, even with him being so old. Of course I got better-looking beaux than him, young fellas, but I thought I'd come in and see him and maybe look for Em too. I went right to his room, and he damn near had a fit. Told me I should never ought of come and I got to go right home. I thought the hell with him, and I went on up to Em's room and then downstairs, figuring I'd get some corfee. When I was in the kitchen I thought I heard somebody, so I come out into the hall. That closet door was open and it stank something awful around there, so I went closer to see what it was, and then she hit me. I know she's a nut. Em told me."

"It doesn't pay to be too positive about these things," Lewis said with some reserve. "Appely denies having asked you to marry him. Do you have the letter in which he proposed to you?"

"Sure, it's in my pocketbook. You got my pocketbook, ain'tcha? Where is it?"

"Oh, yes. It's upstairs in your room. I put it there."

But he had the letter in his pocket, only it was signed merely with a "B" and bore no return address or name on the envelope.

He thought of the handwriting, and suddenly he jumped up from his chair and left the room. He went to Christine's office, shut the door behind him, and pulled out the letter, Em's I.O.U. from Mr. Appely, and the note to Agatha telling her to get Em out of the closet. He placed them side by side on a table and stood looking at them for some time.

Simple enough. The handwriting in the letter was the same as that in the threatening note and in the I.O.U.

Chapter 29

LEWIS went swiftly and quietly up to Mr. Appely's room. He knocked and entered without waiting, but Mr. Appely was not there. The room was untidy, the closet door standing open and drawers gaping, and Lewis gave a grim little nod. He went downstairs again and looked in the doctors' rooms and out on the porch and then walked through to the kitchen.

Fred Slupp was eating his dinner at the table while Agatha cleaned up around him. Mrs. Kroning was doing something at the stove.

Fred buttered a piece of bread and said to Agatha, "I'd like to know, miss, why these Kronings sit like gentry around the dining-room table when it's in the kitchen they should be."

Mrs. Kroning turned slowly from the stove with a look of such deadly menace that Lewis half expected it to raise a rash on the back of Fred's neck. Her voice was low, but it stopped the piece of bread and butter halfway between the table and Fred's mouth.

"If I ever again hear the name of Kroning soiled on your own tongue, Fred Slupp—"

Lewis vastly regretted having to leave in the middle of it, but time and his job were pressing. He slipped into the back lobby where the stairs went up, and down to the cellar, and began a cautious descent. The cellar was dimly lighted, and he kept against the wall and made no noise. He spared only a brief glance at the coalbins, the furnace, and the shadowy corners and worked his way silently to where the old ice chest stood against a wall.

Mr. Appely was there, searching frantically.

"Waste of energy," Lewis observed. "It's gone."

Mr. Appely started violently and then sagged against the box, his mouth working in a futile effort to speak.

"I really don't understand you," Lewis went on. "You have a good business and a comfortable living. Why go to the length of murder to get more money?"

Words came to Mr. Appely in a stuttering rush. "I didn't—I didn't! You don't understand. I didn't kill Em. I couldn't kill anybody. It's only the money, you *must* understand, just the money—"

"I'm willing to understand," Lewis said amiably. "Suppose we go back to your room, and you can tell me all about it."

Mr. Appely gave an eager little gasp, and a trickle of moisture ran from his forehead down the side of his face. "Oh yes, yes, I'll tell you. You must not accuse me of murder—monstrous—simply monstrous."

"Where's the suitcase you probably have with you?" Lewis asked flatly.

Mr. Appely pointed in dumb terror, and Lewis nodded. "Pick it up."

They went up the back stairs to Mr. Appely's room, and Lewis shut the door behind them. Mr. Appely started immediately to tidy the disorder, and Lewis said sharply, "That can wait. Sit down."

Mr. Appely sat down, his eyes pink-rimmed and his forehead glistening. He glanced at Lewis and then looked away quickly.

"I always wanted to expand," he said drearily. "I wish I hadn't now. The store was doing well, but that's what I wanted. I felt that I needed a larger place, more stock and equipment. I knew all about Em and the doctor, and I knew that she was getting money from him. So I—I borrowed from her and opened my new store."

"On three thousand?"

"Oh no, no. I had some of my own and I used that too. She wouldn't give me any more at the time, but she did promise another sum later on, and then when I needed it she refused me. I knew that she kept money around the house, and I began to search, but I could not find it. I was desperate. When you expand that way, you have to expect to pour money in until the thing is properly launched. That—that's why I struck up an acquaintance with the girl, with Ginny. I thought she'd be valuable to know. I might get some money that way, perhaps. And then I received a most dreadful shock, really ghastly. I was searching in the cellar one time, and I saw the—the ghost of the doctor."

Lewis sighed. "I'm a cop, Mr. Appely, and I don't believe in ghosts."

Mr. Appely swallowed twice. "No—no, of course not. I mean, I never believed in such nonsense myself. But I tell you, it was the ghost of the old doctor himself! He always wore evening clothes for dinner, you know—tuxedo—even if he were not going out, and there he was in the cellar, dressed that way. I thought he'd come back to warn me, and I fled to my room. I was terrified. I was too frightened to go on searching for the money for a while, and instead I tried to get it out of Em again. She would not give it to me, though, and she loaned some to that Julia Rost simply to tantalize and annoy me. It was typical of Em, that sort of thing. She loved having power over people. I believe she knew that I was looking for her money, not to steal, you understand, but simply to borrow the sum she had promised me."

"She became afraid of you?"

"No, never. She was afraid of the ghost, even though she said he once moved her money to a safer place. She refused to go down to the cellar because she declared that he was there, and she always said that he was evil and that was why he had to walk. She also said that she was frightened because he sometimes came up from the cellar."

"Why did she tell you all this?"

Mr. Appely sighed and looked down at the toes of his neat little shoes. "She had many ways of changing the subject when I asked for money. These were merely some of her digressions. She would creak back and forth in that rocker of hers with a ouija board in her lap and tell me that she used it to communicate with the doctor and that he was always walking around the cellar. She said that she was afraid only when he came upstairs."

Lewis shook his head a little. "Are you telling me that you believed all that?"

"But I saw him."

"After Em told you about it?"

"Well, yes," Mr. Appely admitted. "But there was no mistake, I assure you."

"O.K. Now tell me how Em died."

"I don't know!" Mr. Appely cried shrilly. "I've told you, I know nothing about it! I just saw her dragging the chair into the closet."

"Who?"

"Miss Agatha. She was trying to hide her after she had killed her. She must have killed her. She always hated her so. She put her in that closet. You could leave someone there forever. It's sealed. She wanted to pretend that Em had left."

"So why didn't you notify the police at once when you saw a body being hidden?"

Mr. Appely's head drooped, and he whispered, "I feared I'd be asked what I was doing down there at such a time."

"No, you didn't," Lewis said. "You wanted to find the money first and ask that girl to marry you, and then you would have been willing to have Em's body discovered. You finally found the money and securities, too, and you put the securities in Em's room and the money in the old icebox in the cellar."

Mr. Appely nodded without raising his eyes.

"After that you sent Miss Agatha a note, supposedly from Em, to get her body out of the closet. I know you wrote that note, but I'm puzzled as to how you can have two such different handwritings. It fooled an expert."

Mr. Appely raised his head, and a faint hint of pride glimmered through his general collapse. "I am left-handed, but I was made to use my right hand when I was a boy. The result is that I can manage quite well with either hand, but the writing is dissimilar. I use my left hand only when I want my identity kept out of it."

Lewis considered it and then nodded. "So why did you write out the I.O.U. for Em?"

Mr. Appely's head sank again, and he fumbled for words.

"Em never required an I.O.U., did she?" Lewis went on. "You wrote that to hide the larger amount she loaned you, since people knew you owed her something. You thought it would make you look like a good, respectable boy when you brought it to light yourself."

Mr. Appely said nothing, and Lewis shifted his weight on Agatha's uncomfortable bedroom chair. "Had you been looking for the money on the night you saw Miss Agatha hide Em in the closet?"

"Yes, I—I'd been looking for some hours. I'd gone upstairs to bed and was just dozing off when I thought of another likely place, so I came down again."

"Didn't it occur to you, after you'd found the money, to take Em out of the closet yourself?"

Mr. Appely said it had, and added almost aggrievedly that the closet door had been locked. "I looked for the key in the drawer where it was kept, but it was not there. I knew then that she had it, and I did not really care. It would have been such a revolting task. *She* had put the body in there. It was up to her to take it out."

"I don't see why it was so important to you to have her found," Lewis said. "You had the money, and no one knew about it."

"It was indecent. No service, no proper burial—"

"And all the rest of the money still lying there. You wanted to marry the girl and bring out the fact that she was Em's daughter."

"Certainly not. I—you have no right to talk to me like that."

"Why not?" Lewis asked coldly, and added, "What made you think that Miss Bunson had the key?"

"It was logical. I waited for her the night I wrote the note—I waited for many hours, and she did not come down until morning. She tried the door but made no attempt to unlock it, and then Dr. Herser appeared, and she hurried away. Dr. Herser tried the door and then turned around suddenly, and I thought she had seen me. I had been peering through that swinging door, you see. I hurried up the back stairs and returned to my room."

"Why did you attack Miss Kroning?" Lewis asked casually.

"But I didn't. I never touched the girl!" Mr. Appely cried excitedly. "I told her to go home at once, and she promised that she would. I did not notice that she had left her bag behind."

Lewis stood up and gratefully kicked back the chair on which he had been sitting. Julia and Christine, who had been trying to listen outside the door, fled precipitately and crowded into the nearest bedroom, which proved to be Allen's. He had been reading in bed, and he dropped the book and pulled the sheet up over his chest. "I am not receiving," he said coldly.

They scarcely noticed him. Christine was saying, "You know, I don't believe he did kill Em. He simply is not the type."

"Why don't you give us a history of the crime?" Allen asked from the bed. "With your knowledge of psychology, acquired and inherent, it should be quite simple for you."

Christine turned and gave him a long, thoughtful stare. "Your irritable sarcasm is childish and should be ignored. But as a matter of fact, I believe I *do* know."

Chapter 29

"CHRISTINE! What are you talking about?" Julia demanded excitedly. "Do you really know what all this is about?"

Christine was peering through a crack of the door. "He's taking him off," she said in a low voice.

Allen took the opportunity to get out of bed and slide into a robe. The two women went out into the hall as Lewis and Mr. Appely descended the stairs, and Allen followed, trying to appear indifferent. Julia went on down, but Christine, after a moment's hesitation, slipped along to Agatha's room. She knocked and after a brief wait turned the knob and went in.

Agatha was in bed. She was a bit startled at the intrusion, but when she saw who it was her head settled into the pillow again.

"How are you feeling?" Christine asked.

"Very well, thank you."

Christine switched on a lamp that stood on the bureau and advanced to the side of the bed. "I have a pill for you."

Agatha turned her head away. "No—no, I really don't need it."

"I think you'd better." Christine sat down on the edge of the mattress. "I know it was quite a shock to hear about your father tonight."

"It doesn't matter," Agatha said, her voice dull. "I'd just like to go to sleep now, please."

Christine looked at her for a moment and then got up and left, a bit reluctantly. Agatha kept her eyes closed until the light had been switched off and the door closed, and then she stared miserably into the darkness. That cheap, common little creature was her sister, actually her sister, and there could never be anything now in her memory of her father but shame. He had always been so smart and elegant and colorful, and he had married a sloppy, dirty woman like Em. But she must put it out of her mind. It didn't matter. Nothing mattered at all. There was no hope anywhere. She hated everything. Go to sleep and get away from it.

Christine went downstairs. She found Julia and Allen in the front hall, and Mirrie and Will were just inside Allen's waiting room. "What happened?" she asked curiously.

"Bigshot Lewis put a ring through little Appely's nose and ast him would he be so kind as to follow on to the slaughter-house, for questioning, *he* sez. Can you tie it? I suppose he ain't been questioning him for the last hour. Maybe he's gonna think up some more on the way down there. Looks like the little guy done it, all right, and him tryin' to make up to our Ginny. If Lewis woulda took his eye off him for one minute, I'da bust him right in his map."

"Where's your mother?" Christine asked. "Is she with Ginny?"

"Yeah, I guess so." Will yawned. "Ma's in bed a'ready. She always hits the hay early, so she can catch the worm in the morning."

"Has Lewis left for the night?"

"I suppose even Lewis goes home occasionally and blows the dust off his bed," Allen said. "Why don't we hole in and try to get some sleep too?"

"Poor Mr. Appely," Christine murmured.

"Why? So many skunks get their little paws caught in traps. He's only another one."

Julia extinguished her cigarette in a card tray that had never before been defaced with ashes. "Christine thinks he's being falsely accused. She has her eye on someone else."

"Oh no," Christine protested. "I—it was only theory. It's a job for the police, nothing to do with me."

Allen gave her a faint smile. "It's really refreshing to hear you speak sense occasionally."

"Yes, it must be. I'm going to bed. Good night." She went off to her room and shut the door firmly behind her.

"Now why did you have to go and make her mad?" Julia demanded pettishly. "I wanted to hear what it is she has under her hat."

"She's too much inclined to rely on what people *should* do under certain circumstances," Allen said, shrugging. "It's dangerous."

Christine's door, behind which she had waited to see whether there would be any remarks, opened abruptly. "I should like so much," she said, emerging, "to stuff those words down your throat that I believe I'll show you a few things around here. Things that you have never even dreamed of because your mind is wrapped up in cotton wool and shut up tightly in a little box with neat labels."

"What do the labels say?" Allen asked, grinning at her.

Christine started up the stairs. "I'll explain things later, making an effort to keep the long words out of it. Right now I'm going to look at my patients."

"Ain't that like a dame?" Will said, gazing after her. "First she's gotta hit the sack right away. Then she gets all steamed up because some guy opens his yap, and nothin' won't do but she's gonna show how much she knows."

"I was just going," Julia said doubtfully, "but now I think I'll wait."

Mirrie adjusted the belt around her neat waist. "Will, I *must* go. It's late, and Mother will worry."

"Hang around, hon. Let's see what gives."

"Don't waste your time," Allen said, heading for the stairs. "Nothing's going to give tonight. I'm going to bed. She can show me tomorrow, or some other time."

"Oh well." Julia made a little face at the other two. "I suppose the front door is open now, and we might as well call it a day."

Mirrie nodded. "Yes. Really, Will."

"O.K." Will heaved himself away from the wall which had been supporting him. "We'll settle for some shuteye. I gotta go to work tomorrow, anyways. Don't want to lose my job now—eh, kid?"

Julia, with a vague idea that the front door might still be locked, gave it a vigorous pull, and it flew back against her. She muttered, "Damn!" called a hasty good night to the other two, and went off before she could be bored by the amorous murmurs that would precede their leave-taking.

Christine went to Ginny's room first. She knocked lightly and walked into darkness and a silence that was broken by Mrs. Kroning's sharp voice.

"Who is it?"

"Dr. Herser. I just wanted to check up on Ginny."

"She's sleepin', leastways, she was before you come in, and me too. If we want you, I'll holler. We don't want to run up no bills that ain't necessary."

"No, certainly not," Christine said coolly. "But Ginny should see her own doctor when she gets home. And there's another thing. You should keep this door locked. After all, someone has attacked her once."

"You stick to your pills, young woman," Mrs. Kroning said, punching her pillow. "It was that crazy little Appely who done all the mischief around here, and they took him away, so we got nothing more to worry about. Get outa here now and leave me sleep."

Christine got out, hoping that between them she and Mrs. Kroning had not awakened Ginny. She stepped on someone's foot and swung around to find Allen, who had been waiting for her.

"Don't apologize. I may not know much about the inner workings of the head, but in my humble way I have devoted some study to the feet. I have no corns."

"Why don't you keep your clumsy, corn-free feet out of my way?"

Allen regarded her with a mild eye. "You've been talking a bit wildly in front of people. I'm sure you'll resent it, but I feel that I should warn you to be careful."

"I've said nothing that was in the least wild. I meant every word of it."

"I think that makes it worse. Would you care to step into my room and explain? The others have gone, but of course they'll spread your remarks around."

Christine was conscious of a sudden prickling of fear, which she tried valiantly to conceal. She regretted her indiscretion, was annoyed with Allen for having identified it as one, and realized that there was nothing left to do but brazen it out. She moved along to Agatha's door and listened, and was not surprised to hear the sounds of restless tossing from within. She sighed, returned to Allen, who had been watching her in silence, and said, "All right. Come on and I'll tell you a few things."

Allen led the way to his room and drew up two chairs. "I doubt whether Agatha would consider this rendezvous a fitting thing for her house. If she found out about it she might turn you out into the snow, because it is always the woman who pays."

"Agatha," said Christine, "has found a doctor who suits her, after fooling along with one who didn't. She won't turn *me* out into the snow."

"That being so, or not, suppose we leave it for the moment. Tell me who killed Em."

"I'll tell it my way," Christine said childishly, "and if you yawn, just once, I'll leave before you get your jaws together again. First of all, Em mentioned more than once that she had seen a ghost."

"Sure. Agatha walking in her sleep."

"Do you think Em was blind?"

"Far from it."

"Then when she saw Agatha walking in her sleep, why would she think it was anything else?"

"Well—" Allen hesitated. "Agatha would look different. Her nightgown—and Em was imaginative—Things like that."

"Things like what? She didn't say it was a woman who looked like Agatha. She said it was the ghost of the old doctor."

"Just talk." Allen shrugged. "It sounded more dramatic. You didn't know Em as well as I did."

"No, of course not, but I've heard a lot about her. I think you're assuming things because it's convenient. It's a common failing."

"So the ghost of the old doctor changed her securities to a safer hiding place."

Christine nodded slowly. "Probably, just that. Mr. Appely was plucking her for all he could get, and maybe Em enjoyed dangling promises of more in front of him. So perhaps he was harried into trying to steal it."

"And the ghost of the doctor further frustrated the poor little man by removing the money to a safer place?"

"Maybe."

"So?"

"So the ghost kills Em and makes a try for Ginny."

"Why?"

"And also makes sure the money is not stolen from Em."

"Again, why?"

Christine raised her shoulders and let them drop. "Possibly the ghost thought the money would revert to Agatha."

"But I happen to know that the weapon used on Ginny was planted in Agatha's room. The ghost tries to get her booked for a murder, and tries to get money for her too?"

Christine nodded. "Yes, that's it. He wants her to have the money and to be blamed for the murder."

Allen rumpled his hair violently. "I'm not sure that I get you. In fact, I don't."

Christine said, "Shh!" sharply and went over to the door. She opened it a crack and after a moment's peering whispered, "There she goes. I thought she would tonight. Agatha's walking again."

Chapter 31

CHRISTINE slid out of the room. She ignored Allen, who hesitated for a moment and then decided to follow her. The heavy carpeting enabled them to go quietly, and they followed Agatha down the stairs. In the lower hall she slowed and came to a stop before a table, where she picked up one of the ornaments. She stood there for a while, holding it in her hand, and then she slowly replaced it.

Christine clutched at Allen's arm and whispered, "That has some meaning."

"Shh."

Agatha moved down the hall to the kitchen, where she switched on the light. Christine and Allen remained outside peering through a crack of the swinging door and fighting silently for the better position. Agatha had shifted out of their line of vision, but she presently came back again, and Allen murmured. "She has the gun in her hand."

Christine saw that she had, but it hung loosely from her fingers as she walked restlessly about the kitchen. As they watched she made suddenly for the sitting room and disappeared inside. They could see a light spring up through the slightly opened door.

Allen urged Christine forward with pressure on her arm, and they advanced to the door of the sitting room. Agatha was speaking in an odd thick voice, and they heard her say, "You can go now. You can go now. You're *rotten*."

There was no sound of anyone else in the room, and Agatha emerged again rather suddenly. Christine and Allen backed precipitately against the wall, but she passed by them without a glance and walked through the kitchen to the cellar stairs. There was a dim light in the cellar, and she went down without hesitation, as though she had a purpose now. Christine and Allen watched her walk straight to the furnace and open the door. There was no fire since the weather had been warm, and she peered in vaguely, the gun still dangling from her hand. She closed the door and straightened up, and then leaned down to open it and look in once more.

Christine and Allen stood in obscurity against the stone wall, and as they watched in silence there was the sound of a step on the stairs above them. They stared up, remaining still and almost breathless, and they saw a man descend into the dim light. He was dressed in a dinner jacket with stiff-bosomed shirt and black tie, and he seemed to have a small mustache, although his face was not clear in the shadows. He carried a cigarette in a holder, with an air of ease and negligence, and he wore gloves.

Christine breathed, "The ghost!" and felt Allen's hand tighten on her arm.

Agatha caught sight of the man as he advanced, and became very still. Her eyes never left his face, and at last she said faintly, "You're rotten."

The man was standing directly in front of her now, and he pointed silently to the gun and then extended his hand, palm upward.

Agatha retreated a step. "No—no! I'm going to throw it away. I must find a place—"

The man advanced and closed the distance between them, his palm still extended. Agatha stood rigid, her mouth a little open and the gun still dangling uncertainly in her hand—but she made no move to give it to him. He leaned toward her, gently loosened it from her fingers, and turned abruptly, holding it in his own hand. He made for the stairs and went up without haste. Christine and Allen glanced at each other and without words agreed to abandon Agatha and follow this suave ghost.

Agatha awakened as they were creeping up the stairs. She looked at them vaguely, blinking and trying to orient herself, and then realization dampened her with shame. She had been walking in her sleep again, with only her nightgown and a thin robe, and they had seen her. She drew a heavy breath and was conscious of the deep depression that settled on her whenever she had been walking. She always knew, even if she woke up in bed, and she always dreamed of her father. He'd be there in his dinner jacket, which had been his usual costume for the evening whether he went out or not. She'd had to change into a long black dress, too, with the garnet necklace her mother had left her. He'd sneered at the dress, of course, but he'd never given her money enough to get anything decent.

She belted her robe securely and moved away from the furnace. She must go at once, get upstairs without being seen. But she was not so frightened this time. She'd looked him in the face and told him he was rotten, and he was. Dressing up every evening and waving a cigarette holder around couldn't cover up the evil inside. And he *was* evil.

She went up to the kitchen, gripping her robe tightly around her spare body. She had always thought her father so dashing and smart, mean, certainly, but dashing and smart. Yet what was so dashing about having anything to do with a creature like Em? Em might have been better-looking eighteen years ago, but she had always been dirty and sloppy too.

She started and crouched back against the wall as she heard someone come in the front door, but whoever it was went straight up the stairs. She breathed freely again and then set her teeth together in impotent fury. It was just too much, people coming in and out of the house this way. Of course with boarders you had to expect a certain amount of it, but one thing was certain—she had made up her mind. Mr. Appely would have to go. Making up to that young girl. Really disgusting.

She decided to go up the back stairs and went to the lobby, closing the door carefully behind her. It was very dark as she started up, and she went slowly, clutching the handrail. There was a streak of light at the top, and she frowned as she realized that someone must have left the door slightly ajar up there. It should be closed. She hated doors hanging open—so untidy. Anyway, the boarders were supposed to use the front stairs. Perhaps Mrs. Kroning had gone up this way. No. One of the first things she had said was that she never used anyone's back stairs. One of the others, then—that Christine? She was careless, but nice, though. It was good to have a lady doctor in the house.

Her felt slippers made no noise as she ascended, but she stopped about halfway up as she heard the sound of voices in the upstairs hall. They were speaking quietly. Who was it? Dr. Gremson? And Christine. Someone else. It was that Lewis. She didn't like him, although he had been courteous to her at all times. Her face grew hot at the thought of him, all the things he knew about her, and she had wept in front of him! Tears seeped from her eyes again. All this dreadful trouble. Why had she done it, moved Em like that? She always dreamed while she was walking, but she would know if she had hurt Em, and she hadn't. What had she been dreaming about on that awful night? She had seen Em, and Em was laughing at her, and then she had gone to the cellar and seen her father, and she had given him the gun as he asked. He always asked for the gun in these dreams. Not by words, he never spoke, but by gestures. Why did she bring that gun down when she was sleepwalking? It happened frequently, and sometimes she brought handkerchiefs and other little things and put them in the sitting room. When she had the gun, she always dreamed that her father asked for it, and she always gave it to him, all without words. Then he would return it to her, and usually she took it back upstairs, but not always. On that dreadful night he'd taken it from her in the cellar and gone away, and she had returned to her room. She had seen Em when she passed through the kitchen, and then when she woke up in her room, she had known at once that something was wrong with Em.

The voices in the upper hall were receding, and presently they were shut behind the door of a room. Agatha started to mount, and stopped again immediately, her hand frozen on the rail. The crack of light above her was widening.

Agatha remained motionless, even her breath suspended, and as the door swung open she saw a slight figure, arrayed in the black and white of evening dress, step out into the hall above.

He disappeared at once, and Agatha put a hand to her damp forehead. Was she imagining things, or still asleep? She saw him only in her sleep, as part of a dream. But he'd been there, at the top of the stairs, and she was not asleep now. She knew she was awake. Her father was dead, and she did not believe in ghosts or visitations. What was it? What was happening?

She forced her trembling legs up the rest of the stairs and clenched her teeth to stop their chattering. She must follow him, must find out. She saw Christine and Allen standing outside Ginny's room, but Lewis was not with them. They did not see her, and she pressed into the shadows against the wall. Where was he, that man? Her father. No, it couldn't be. Her father was dead.

Suddenly there were voices from Ginny's room, the sound of a struggle and a cry from Mrs. Kroning. Christine and Allen ran in, and Agatha moved forward on stiff shaking legs. She looked through the open door into the lighted room and saw Ginny sitting up in bed, her eyes round and terrified. Mrs. Kroning was struggling into a robe and asking excitedly, "What *is* this? What's goin' on here?"

The man was there, slim and straight in his black suit and white shirt, and Lewis had his arm in a firm grip.

"Who *is* he?" Allen asked.

Agatha moved closer, and was suddenly shaking with fury.

"How *dare* you wear my father's clothes, Fred Slupp!"

Chapter 32

AGATHA was back in bed, her body stretched between smooth sheets. Christine had insisted, and had made her take a pill too. The pill was of no use. She would never be able to sleep. Fred Slupp, walking around every night in her father's clothes, with a false mustache and her father's old cigarette holder. Smoking real cigarettes too, a thing he had never done in the daytime. So he must have dropped that ash in the drawer when he took the key, and he must have wondered why the closet door was locked and where Em's body had disappeared to. Perhaps he hadn't thought that far. The body was gone and that was that. And he had put his plants in there! Agatha shuddered.

He had always liked things to be neat and orderly, and so it must have pleased him, when his work was done, to dress up and pretend to be her father. He had a great respect for what he called the gentry. He had had the impudence to say that the mustache was not an attempt to ape her father. He merely thought it went well with evening clothes. Apparently he had even taken walks in the neighborhood dressed that way.

Agatha heaved an impatient sigh and turned over, and Christine, just outside the door, shook her head a little. She ought to be asleep by now. She was a tough one, but she'd surely go off soon.

Allen came up the stairs bearing a tray on which reposed a pot of coffee, cups, and saucers. He raised his eyebrows at Christine and jerked his head toward his room, and she nodded. She lingered for a moment at Agatha's door, and when she turned at last to go to Allen's room, she found that she was accompanied by Mrs. Kroning and Ginny. Allen tried to look these two out again, but Mrs. Kroning said merely, "A good hot cuppa corfee is what we all need."

Ginny sighed. "It'll do if you ain't got no gin. I sure need something after what I been through, him tryin' to hit me like that again."

"I have only two cups," Allen said austerely.

Mrs. Kroning nodded. "Yeah, I see. You better hunt up two more for you and your young woman."

Allen looked rather helplessly around the room and eventually produced two silver mugs that he had received as an infant in celebration of his christening.

Mrs. Kroning and Ginny took the two chairs, Christine established herself on a stool, and Allen, after another look around the room, sat on the end of the bed.

Mrs. Kroning took a loud sip of coffee and sighed contentedly. "Now whoever woulda thought that scraggly little Fred Slupp was a murderer?"

Ginny shivered. "Why did he try to get me? I never done nothin' to him."

"I don't think he'd have bothered about you if you hadn't come here," Christine said. "But when he saw you, he was enraged at the possibility that you might have come to stay. He knew you were Em's daughter, and he didn't want you here. You were very fortunate that he half missed when he hit you. He knows where to hit, and he got Em on the right spot."

"May I be permitted a question?" Allen asked.

"Sure." Mrs. Kroning gave him an amiable nod. "Go ahead."

"Why did he want Em out of the house? And Ginny?"

"Perhaps the same reason that Agatha had," Christine said slowly. "Em's sloppy ways. Agatha could not murder, so she was frustrated to the point where her health was damaged, and of course there was an old trouble there too—her father's constant sneers. In her disturbed condition she was walking frequently in her sleep, and of course she ran across Fred dressed in her father's clothes. She naturally thought she was dreaming of her father."

"Does he look so much like her father?" Allen asked.

"Well, Agatha says that the figure is about the same, and the mustache identical. His hair is iron-gray and so was the doctor's, and when he dressed up he slicked it down as the doctor wore his. Fred had an intense admiration for the doctor's elegance and apparently got a tremendous pleasure out of dressing up and aping him, the same clothes, the cigarette holder, the mustache. He did wander around a bit, but I think he stuck to the cellar for the most part. Another thing, most of Agatha's light bulbs are fairly dim, I suppose to save electricity, so that she could never have seen Fred very clearly when he was pretending to be her father."

"What type would you call Fred?" Allen asked politely. "I am very skillful at flinging sticking plaster around, but the little wheels that go around inside the head are apt to confuse me."

"Now don't you feel bad, Doc," Mrs. Kroning said soothingly. "I'm sure you're real smart about lots of things, but this here lady doctor, she knows that new stuff—you know, fizzyatry."

"Yes." Allen nodded. "I believe she was head of the fizzyatry class."

"Just a natural talent," Christine murmured modestly. "But Fred's type—" She glanced at Allen. "Don't type anybody. He is mentally slow and a hard worker with his hands. He is never satisfied unless what he is doing is done exactly right. Agatha is the same, and your nurse, Mirrie. Everything must be exactly so. They are the same that far, but after that they vary. Mirrie is fastidious about her person, but she goes in for style too. She wants to live. Agatha is clean about her person, but she lives for her house and allows others to ruin her chance of living for herself. Fred had no friends of his own. He lived in the doings of the house, associated himself with it and with the people who lived here. When Agatha in her sleep believed him to be her father, he began more and more to believe it himself."

"You still ain't told us why he wanted to get rid of me," Ginny said in an injured voice.

"Yes, I did. You were an interloper, Em's daughter, and you threatened the security of the house."

"Some nerve!" Mrs. Kroning said indignantly, having misunderstood the meaning of the word "interloper." "I hope they fix him good."

"Ginny ought to be in bed," Christine said, shifting on her uncomfortable stool.

Mrs. Kroning nodded and heaved herself up from her chair. "That's right. Come on, Ginny, right away, and I don't want no arguments."

Christine went out with them, said good night at their door, and went on downstairs to her own rooms. She was considering throwing herself onto the couch in her clothes and going to sleep that way, when there was a tap on the door, and Allen walked in. She groaned loudly, and he said, "I know you're tired, but you made some wild statements that you were going to explain to me later, and this is later."

Christine fell into a chair and reached for a cigarette. "Well, there were things I noticed. Appely was not out to kill. He's all wrapped up in his shop, and he needed money for it. He'd work at getting the money, but he wouldn't go as far as murder. Julia needs money too, all the time, and I'll bet she got some from Em, but she wouldn't have anything in writing. Also, she'd be more apt to shrug and go bankrupt than kill to keep going. Mirrie would have liked Em out of the way so that Will could inherit, but Mirrie is cagey, and she could wait. Agatha, of course, was desperate to be rid of Em—all that mess when she was trying to keep things clean—but a lot of people would like to get rid of a lot of people without going as far as murder."

Allen nodded gravely. "I was not head of my fizzyatry class, but I do know that. Only, why did Fred kill? He wanted Em out of the way, of course, but he'd wanted that for a long time."

"You were living here, and yet you didn't really notice Fred. There's something else that you've all overlooked. Em was married long ago to someone who disappeared and never showed up again. There was no mention of a divorce, and presumably she married the doctor without bothering about it, and he didn't know."

"He must have known."

"Did you know?" Christine asked.

"Well, no, but—"

"But nothing. Agatha didn't know either, or she would have said something. As it was, she merely passed out with shame instead. I asked Will about it, and he told me, but you can understand why none of the Kronings brought it up tonight. But Fred must have known. It is the reason that Em didn't stand up for her rights when the doctor kept the marriage a secret and paid her off quietly. She wasn't so stupid that she didn't know she could have a lot more if she took her rightful place as the doctor's wife. She was afraid to insist. Just tonight Fred made a remark about the Kronings, said they should be eating in the kitchen but didn't add, with him. I was standing at the door of the kitchen and so were you. You merely laughed, but I thought it was significant for Fred to tell Agatha where the Kronings should eat. In other words, Fred had ceased to just ape the doctor. He *was* the doctor, and the first thing he had to do was to get rid of the woman who had married him when she was already married to someone else. She'd made a fool of him, and he'd never liked her, anyway. When the daughter appeared, he was afraid she had come to stay, so he tried to get rid of her too. Later tonight, after hearing all that talk at the table, he *had* to wipe her out. If he did away with her, the other Kronings wouldn't come into his house. So Agatha conveniently turned up with the gun in her hand. If she hadn't, he would have got something else and planted it in her room after he had killed Ginny, as he did with the wrench after his first attack on the girl. There were no fingerprints on that wrench because he always wore the doctor's gloves. They made him feel more elegant. He was going to blame Agatha for everything. That had been the doctor's way, and now he was the doctor and would do the same."

"It's fantastic," Allen muttered. "Did you know it was Fred when he appeared in the basement?"

"Oh yes. As soon as I heard talk of a ghost, the doctor's ghost, I looked around to see who could possibly fit the role, and Fred was the only one. It didn't seem probable, but I listened to what he said, after that. Just a few little things, but for a supposedly humble character Fred was getting rather bold. I knew something was wrong with him."

Someone came in the front door, and they both got up and peered out into the hall. It was Lewis, and though he looked tired, there was an air of triumph about him.

"I dropped in on my way back to relieve Miss Bunson's mind on one point at least. Seems that this Em's marriage was bigamous, so Miss Bunson needn't worry about sharing her house with the girl. You can tell her, if you will. That Slupp fellow is nuts, I guess. He's been yelling that his daughter, Agatha, is crazy and should be put away. Says she's going around killing people. The poor dope thinks he's the doctor himself."

Allen said, "I don't know whether I like your news or not."

"Huh? Listen, I'm dead on my feet. I'm going home to bed. Thanks for all the help you've given me."

Christine smiled at him. "Why did you tell Mr. Appely that Ginny had killed Em?"

Lewis hid a yawn behind a polite hand. "I found her purse in his room and I was trying to get him talking, but the cold haddock just acted surprised. Good night. Thanks again."

They closed the door after him, and Allen turned to Christine, with one eyebrow elevated.

She gave a tearing yawn and muttered, "You know something? I was only fooling. I don't know anything about fizzyatry."

"Ah, shut up," Allen said, rumpling his hair. "Look, if you'll leave all that stuff to the boys with brains, in future, and stay with the sticking plaster, I might let you have that gorgeous ring I promised you years ago."

"O.K., hand it over. It'll come in handy for pawning when I get hungry."

THE END

If you enjoyed this book, ask your bookseller for the other Constance and Gwenyth Little books reprinted by The Rue Morgue, as well as for other titles in our vintage mystery reprint program. To suggest titles to reprint or to get our catalog call 800-699-6214, or go to our web page:
www.ruemorguepress.com
or write:
The Rue Morgue Press
P.O. Box 4119
Boulder, CO 80306